Idol, Burning

Idol, Burning

A Novel

Rin Usami

Translated by Asa Yoneda

HarperVia

An Imprint of HarperCollinsPublishers

HarperCollins books may be purchased for educational, business, or sales
promotional use. For information, please email the Special Markets Department
at SPsales@harpercollins.com.

Originally published as *Oshi, moyu* in Japan in 2020 by Kawade Shobo Shinsha.

FIRST HARPERVIA EDITION PUBLISHED IN 2022

Designed by Terry McGrath
Illustrations © Leslie Hung

Library of Congress Cataloging-in-Publication Data

Names: Usami, Rin, 1999- author. | Yoneda, Asa, translator.
Title: Idol, burning : a novel / Rin Usami ; translated by Asa Yoneda.
Other titles: Oshi, moyu. English
Description: First edition. | New York, NY : HarperVia, 2022. | "Originally published
  as Oshi, moyu in Japan in 2020 by Kawade Shobo Shinsha"
Identifiers: LCCN 2022009848 | ISBN 9780063213289 (hardcover) | ISBN
  9780063213296 (trade paperback) | ISBN 9780063213302 (ebook)
Subjects: LCGFT: Novels.
Classification: LCC PL876.5.S265 O8413 2022 | DDC 895.63/6—dc23/eng/20220311
LC record available at https://lccn.loc.gov/2022009848

22 23 24 25 26   LSC   10 9 8 7 6 5 4 3 2 1

Idol, Burning

My *oshi* was on fire. Word was he'd punched a fan. No details had emerged yet, but even with zero verification the story had blown up overnight. I'd slept badly. Maybe it was my gut telling me something was up—I woke up, checked the time on my phone, and noticed the commotion in my DMs. My dazed eyes lit on the line

< They're saying Masaki punched a fan >

For a split second I didn't know what was real. The backs of my thighs were sticky with sweat. Once I'd checked the news sites, there was nothing I could do but to sit transfixed on my bed, which had shed its blanket in the night, and watch the fallout as the rumor and the flaming proliferated. The only thing on my mind was the status of my oshi.

< evth ok? >

The text notification popped up on my lock screen, covering up my oshi's eyes like a criminal. It was from Narumi. The words were the first thing out of her mouth the next morning when she ran onto the train car.

"Everything okay?"

Narumi sounded the same in person as she did online. I looked at her face, the round eyes and concerned brows overflowing with tragedy, and thought, *There's an emoji like that.*

"It's not looking good," I said.

"No?"

"Yeah."

The top two buttons of her uniform blouse were open and she sat down next to me in a waft of cold citrus antiperspirant. Social media—which I'd opened almost by reflex after entering 0-8-1-5, my oshi's birthday, into the lock screen, ghostly under the sharp glare—was mired in people's hot breath.

"How bad is it?"

Narumi leaned over and pulled out her phone. There was a dark-toned Polaroid sandwiched inside its clear silicone cover.

"You got Instax!"

"Isn't it great?" Narumi said, with a smile as uncomplicated as a LINE sticker. Everything Narumi said was straightforward, and her facial expressions changed like she was switching out profile pictures. I didn't think she was being fake or insincere; she was just trying to simplify herself as much as possible.

"How many did you get?"

"Ten!"

"Whoa! Wait, but that's only ten thou?"

"When you think of it that way, right?"

"It's worth it. Total steal."

The indie idol group she followed let fans take photos with their favorite group member after live shows. Narumi's showed her with her hair carefully braided and her oshi's arm around her, or the two of them cheek to cheek. Until last year she'd supported a major label group, but now she talked about leaving the mainstream idols on their pedestals and getting up close and personal with the underground. *Come over to the dark side*, she'd say. It's so much better. They remember who you are, and you could get to talk one-on-one, or even date them.

The idea of making direct contact with my oshi didn't interest me. I went to shows, but only to be part of the crowd. I wanted to be inside the applause, inside the screaming, and anonymously post my thanks online afterward.

"So when we hugged, he tucked my hair behind my ear, and I was like, Shit, is there something on it?" Narumi lowered her voice. "And then he said, 'You smell good.'"

"No. Way." I emphasized the pause between the words.

Narumi said, "I know, right? There's just no going back," and slipped the Instax back in her phone cover. Last year, her previous oshi had announced he was retiring from the entertainment industry to go study abroad. She hadn't come to school for three days.

"True," I said.

The shadow of a utility pole passed across our faces. As if to suggest she'd gotten overexcited, Narumi straightened out her knees and, much more calmly, addressed her rosy knee-caps. "Anyway, Akari, you're doing good. It's good you're still here."

"Here like on the way to school?"

"Yeah."

"For a second I thought you meant, among the living."

Narumi laughed somewhere deep inside her chest. "That too."

"Oshi work is life and death."

Fandom talk could get a little over the top.

< Thank you for being born >

< missed out on tickets my life is over >

< he looked at me!! MY FUTURE HUSBAND <3 >

Narumi and I could be guilty of this, too, but it didn't feel right to me to talk marriage and whatnot only when things were going well, so I typed:

< I stan by my oshi in sickness and in health. >

The train came to a stop, and the sound of cicadas swelled. I tapped Post. An instant Like flew in from next to me.

I'd accidentally brought my backpack to school without unpacking it from when I went to see my oshi perform a few days ago. The only things in there I could use for school were the loose-leaf paper and pens I used for noting down my impressions of the show, so I had to share in Classics and borrow for Math, and stand by the side of the pool during PE because I didn't have my swimsuit.

I never noticed it when I was in the pool, but the water overflowing onto the tile felt slick, as though something was dissolved in it—not sweat or sunscreen, but something more abstract, like flesh. The water lapped at the feet of the students sitting out the class. The other student was a girl from the homeroom next to mine. She stood at the very edge of the pool handing out kickboards, wearing a thin white long-sleeved hoodie over her summer uniform. Bare legs gave off blinding flashes of white each time they kicked up a spray of water.

The herd of water-dark swimsuits also looked slippery. The girls pulled themselves up by the silver handrail or onto the grainy yellow ledge, making me think of seals and dolphins and orcas hauling themselves onstage at an aquarium show. Rivulets fell from the cheeks and upper arms of the line of girls saying "Thanks" as they took my pile of kickboards, leaving dark stains on the dry pastel foam. Bodies were so heavy. Legs spraying up water were heavy, and wombs that shed their lining every month were heavy. Kyoko, who was by far the youngest of the teachers, demonstrated "moving from the thighs," using her arms as legs and rubbing them together. "I see some of you just flapping your feet around. None of that effort is getting you anywhere."

We also had Kyoko for Health. She used words like "ovum" and "erectile tissue" without skipping a beat so things never got awkward, but I still felt the burden of my involuntary role as a mammal dragging me down.

In the same way that a night of sleep put wrinkles in a bedsheet, just being alive took a toll. To talk to someone you had to move the flesh on your face. You bathed to get rid of the grime that built up on your skin and clipped your nails because they kept growing. I exhausted myself trying to achieve the bare minimum, but it had never been enough. My will and my body would always disengage before I got there.

The school nurse recommended I go see a specialist, and I was given a couple of diagnoses. The medication made me feel ill, and after I repeatedly no-showed on appointments, even getting to the clinic started to be a struggle. The name they put to the heaviness in my body made me feel better at first, but I also felt myself leaning on it, dangling from it. Only through chasing my oshi could I escape the heaviness just for a moment.

My very first memory is of looking directly up at a figure in green. My oshi, at twelve years old, is playing the role of Peter Pan. I am four. You could say my life started when I saw my oshi fly past overhead, suspended on wires.

But it wasn't until a lot later that he became my oshi. I'd just started high school and had stayed home from a rehearsal for the sports day in May. My hands and feet were sticking out from under a terry blanket. Rough, papery tiredness caught on my overgrown toenails. From outside, the faint sounds of baseball practice landed in my ears. I sensed my awareness lift half an inch into the air at each impact.

The PE clothes I'd washed two days ago in readiness for the rehearsal were nowhere to be found. At six a.m., half-dressed in my school blouse, I'd searched my room, turning it upside down, then given up and fled back to sleep. The next thing I knew, it was noon. Nothing had changed. My ransacked room was like the dishwashing sink at the restaurant I worked at—totally unmanageable.

I cast around under my bed and found a dusty green DVD case. It was the production of *Peter Pan* I'd been taken to see when I was a child. I fed it into the player and the title screen lit up in full color. Occasionally, a line would move across the image. The disc might have been a little scratched.

The first thing I feel is pain. A momentary piercing sensation, and then a pain kind of like being shoved, the force of it. A boy puts his hands on a windowsill and sneaks through the window. When he lets his dangling feet swim inside the room, the tips of his short boots thrust themselves into my heart and carelessly kick upward. *I know this pain*, I think. At my age, my freshman year of high school, pain should be something long buried, something that's become part of my flesh over the years and only prickles once in a while as a reminder. But here it is, just the same as when I was four years old and a small stumble would immediately leave me in tears. Feeling returns to my body as though radiating from that one point of pain, and color and light pour into the grainy image, bringing the world to life. The small green form runs lightly over to the bed where the girl lies, and taps her on the shoulder. Shakes her. *Hey*, the clear, innocent voice rings out. It's Peter Pan. I know, without a doubt, that this is the boy who flew over my head that day.

There was a willful gleam in Peter Pan's eyes, and he took all his lines at a run, like he was trying to convince you of something. He intoned every line the same way. His voice was unvaried, his gestures exaggerated, but the sight of him working so hard just to draw breath and speak made me inhale with him and breathe out powerfully. I was trying to become him. When he ran around the stage, my pale, lazy thighs twitched from the inside. I watched him cry after the dog tore off his shadow and wanted to scoop him up in my arms, together with the sadness that had transmitted itself from him to me. My heart softened, and sent out a heavy flow of blood that pulsed and carried heat through me. Impossible to disperse, the heat pooled in my fists and my folded thighs. I saw him recklessly swing his slender sword until he was backed into a corner, and each time his opponent's weapon grazed his flank I felt a cold blade against my insides. At the stern of the ship, he pushed the captain into the sea and looked up, and when I saw the unchildlike iciness of his gaze, something like a shiver went up my spine. I heard myself groan. Internally, I put it into words: *Shit. Stone cold. That kid could definitely cut off the captain's left hand and feed it to the alligators.* Knowing there was no one home, I tried saying it out loud. "Shit. Stone cold." Then I got carried away and said, "I wanna go to Neverland," and nearly talked myself into wanting it for real.

In the play, Peter Pan kept saying, "I don't wanna grow up." He said it when he left on his adventure, and when he came back and brought Wendy and the rest of them home. The line landed in the core of me and cracked me open. It reconfigured a sequence of words I'd retraced with my ears for so many years without really thinking about it. *I don't wanna grow up. Let's go to Neverland.* Heat gathered at the tip of my nose. *Those words are for me,* I thought. My throat resonated in sympathy, emitting a thin sound. Heat pooled at the corners of my eyes. The words the boy was spitting from his red lips were trying to drag the same words out of me. Instead of words, tears spilled out. I felt that someone was telling me that it was okay to feel heavy at the prospect of growing up, of shouldering weight. The shadows of others who carried that same burden seemed to rise up through his small body. I was connected with him, and, through him, I was also connected with everybody who stood on the other side.

Peter Pan kicked off the stage, spilling golden glitter from his hands as he ascended into the air. I recovered the sensation of four-year-old me jumping off the ground after seeing that production.

I am in the garage at my grandparents' house, and the air is thick with the distinctive smell of the fish mint that grew lushly around it in summer. I sprinkle myself with the "fairy dust" I'd asked for at the gift shop and jump into the air three times, four.

Each time I land on the ground, the air is expelled from the soles of the shoes I was made to wear as a young child, and they give off a loud squeak.

I never believed I could fly. But some part of me was waiting for the pauses between the sounds to get longer and longer, until eventually the sounds stopped altogether. While I was in the air, my body was weightless, and that same lightness was still somewhere inside my sixteen-year-old body, sitting in front of the TV in nothing but my underwear and my school blouse.

The DVD case I find myself reaching for says "MASAKI UENO" in a rounded font. When I search his name, it comes up with a face I've seen a few times on TV. *That's him.* A breeze blows through the new leaves and winds up the spring of my internal clock, which has been running slowly as of late. I get moving. My PE clothes are still nowhere to be found, but there's an inviolable column rising up through the core of me, and I think to myself: *I can do this.*

The internet told me Masaki Ueno was currently a member of the idol group Maza Maza. Recent headshots showed the twelve-year-old boy had shed his chubby cheeks and turned into a young man with a self-assured air. I watched footage of his shows, his movies, his TV dramas. His voice and his body were different now, of course, but the keen gaze he revealed at odd moments, as though he was glaring at something from the very depths of his eyes, was unchanged. When my eyes met his, they reminded me how to really see. I felt an enormous swell of pure energy, neither positive nor negative, come rising up from my very foundation, and suddenly remembered what it felt like to be alive.

*

I caught a glimpse of something similar in the clip that was posted at one p.m. today. Students came back from swimming with wet towels slung over their shoulders, wafting chlorine. The sound of chair legs scraping across the floor and footsteps running swiftly down the hallway rang out in the deserted classroom, marking the start of lunch break. I sat down at a desk in the second row and adjusted my earbuds. My insides tensed up at the imperfect silence.

The video starts with my oshi emerging from the front door of his management's building. Exposed by the flash of camera lights, he looks exhausted.

"Can I ask you a question?" someone says, and holds out a microphone.

"Uh huh."

"Is it true you punched one of your fans?"

"Uh huh."

"How did that happen?"

Here, his tone—which up to then has been so steady you can hardly tell whether he's responding or just nodding along—falters slightly.

"It's a private matter to be resolved between the parties involved. I apologize for any trouble I've caused."

"How about apologizing to her?"

"I already have."

"Will you be stepping back from your work?"

"For now, I don't know. I'm discussing it with my management and the rest of the group."

As he tries to get into the car, a reporter asks angrily, "Are you sorry at all?"

When my oshi turns his head, I think I see, for a split second, some intense emotion in his eyes. But he immediately says, "Something like that."

The car drives off, leaving behind a reflection of the huddle of equipment and people mirrored along its side.

< Who the fuck does he think he is? >

< Learn your lesson and come back soon! We're here for you Masaki! >

< tfw you won't take the L >

< Why doesn't he just explain what actually happened? He's only hurting himself. >

< I've been going to his shows for years but I'm done. If you're a brainwashed cult follower victim-bashing the woman you're not right in the head. >

In the comments section, which was lighting up with new takes, one was rising to the top:

< LIKE ↓↓↓ if you think he has DV perp face ↓↓↓ >

When I reached the end, I replayed the clip and copied out the exchange on a piece of loose-leaf. My oshi must have chosen his words intentionally, because in his fan club newsletter, he'd once answered an interview question by saying he tried not to use phrases like "maybe," "for now," "kind of." I compiled every word my oshi uttered on TV or radio and filed them in a series of binders that took up a small corner of my room. I bought three copies of every CD, DVD, and photo book: one to lend to others, one for personal use, and one to keep. I recorded and re-watched every broadcast. This collection existed to enable me to try to understand my oshi. I'd started blogging my ideas, and pretty soon I was getting more and more comments and shares, and even readers who called themselves fans of my blog and subscribed to updates.

There were as many styles of fandom as there were fans. Some people worshipped every move their oshi made, while others thought discernment made the true fan. There were those who had a romantic interest in their oshi but no interest in their oshi's work; others who had no such feelings but sought a direct connection through engaging on social media; people who enjoyed their oshi's output but didn't care about the gossip; those who found fulfillment in supporting the oshi financially; others who valued being part of a fan community.

My angle was simply to keep trying to understand him, as a person and as an artist. I wanted to see the world through his eyes.

When had I first started feeling this way? I looked back through my blog posts, and the answer seemed to be about a month after my first Maza Maza concert last year. I'd written up a radio appearance, and there was a certain level of demand for the content, maybe because it had only been broadcast regionally, so it was the fifth or sixth most-read post on my blog.

Good morning! Did you catch my oshi on the radio yesterday? It was a great segment, but since I hear it was only on the waves here in Kanagawa, I'm going to note down some of the parts I found the most interesting for all of you who didn't get a chance to hear it. This is a transcript of his answer to the question "What was your first impression of the industry?" The red text is the radio host, Imamura, and blue is Masaki.

"Not good . . ."

"Now I really want to know. Get it off your chest!"

"I remember it pretty clearly. It's my fifth birthday, and my mom says, we're going to the studio, you're going to be on TV now. Out of nowhere. So I get taken onto this set, and it's like a dream. There's a blue sky with clouds and a pastel rainbow, except offstage where the adults are running around it's pitch dark, and my mom's there behind all that black equipment in a houndstooth dress, doing this . . . waving her hands down by her chest. She's only fifteen feet away, but it feels like she's saying goodbye. I'm about to burst into tears, but then the big bear mascot comes up to me and goes like this, you know?"

"Oh—*SHUWATCH*, like Ultraman? No miming, we're on radio."

"Oops. [Laughter.] So the bear's doing the pose and looking down at me with its shiny black eyes. And I want to cry, but I don't—I laugh. I see my smile reflected in the bear's eyes, and it's just perfect. So from then on, the bear keeps doing that move, to make me laugh. And that's how I learned—*oh, okay, no one can tell if your smile is fake*. No one sees how I feel."

"At five years old?"

"Yeah, I'm five."

"That's pretty cynical. [Laughter.]"

"I mean, I get letters, these kids saying, I've been your fan for however many years, since I was this age, or telling me all about themselves, what's going on in their life. And I appreciate it, I really do, it's just—there's a gap there, you know?"

"How could they understand? It's not like they get to see all of you, Masaki."

"But the people around you don't get it, either. No matter who you talk to. I'm always like, *Wow, he just nodded at what I said even though he has no clue what I mean.*"

"Hold on, are you talking about me?"

"That's not what I'm . . . Okay, maybe. You're good at telling people what they want to hear."

"I can't believe you said that. I'm always 100 percent serious, I'm telling you. [Laughter.]"

"I'm sorry. [Laughter.] Anyway, maybe that's the reason I write lyrics and things. Hoping there's one person out there who'll get it. See through to me. Why else would I put myself in the public eye?"

Friends, I finally *felt* what it means to get choked up at something. As I think I've written here before, the first time I saw my oshi live was when he was only twelve, so maybe I'm particularly interested when he speaks about his child actor days. He draws people toward him so strongly, and yet, at the same time, there's something about him that pushes us away. I want to see the world he sees, feel what he feels—what he insists that "no one understands." Even if it takes years, even if I never fully "get it." He has a way of doing that to people—it's his superpower.

It had been a year since I'd made him my oshi. Having spent that time collating as much as I could of the vast quantity of data he'd put out over the past twenty years, I could now predict most of his responses at fan meet Q&As. Watching a performance from such a distance that the performers' faces were invisible to the naked eye, I could tell him apart by the aura around him as he stepped onto the stage. And once, when his bandmate Mina tweeted on my oshi's account as a prank, I replied,

< What's going on? This doesn't sound like Masaki . . . >

Mina responded, saying,

< You busted me lol. I thought my impression was pretty good. >

It was rare for them to address a fan directly. Looking back, that was probably when people started to know me as a Masaki superfan.

Once in a while, my oshi would reveal an unexpected side of himself. I'd try to make sense of it. *Has something changed? Or has he always been this way?* When I worked it out, I'd write it up on my blog. My theory of him would grow more complete.

This incident was different. From what I knew of my oshi, he wasn't a peaceable person. He had his sanctum, and he got annoyed when people tried to step into it. But his reaction was always contained inside his eyes, and he'd never make any kind of visible scene. He never forgot himself—couldn't, even if he tried. He spoke openly about keeping a distance between himself and others. So I found it hard to believe he would ever hit a fan, no matter how much what they'd said had touched a nerve.

I didn't yet know what to think. Most of the fans I'd seen online seemed to be going through the same thing. I wasn't sure whether I should be angry, or coming to his defense, or looking on from a distance at the people getting emotionally invested. I didn't know, but in not knowing, I had a vivid sensation of pressure on my solar plexus. The only thing that seemed sure was that he was still my oshi.

The sound of the school bell took hold of my attention and shook it from side to side, and I felt the clamminess at the back of my neck, the sweat I hadn't even noticed collecting. People came in from lunch and found their seats, complaining about how hot the classroom was, and I knew I had more heat built up under my blouse than any of them, but before I could let it out the door opened. The teacher, Tadano, passed out stacks of handouts, saying "We're all doing our part for 'Cool Biz,' of course," to explain the lack of his usual tan jacket and loud patterned tie. The boy in the seat in front of mine waved a stack of sheets in the air, and I took one and passed it back. The lecture went over my head. I gazed at the handwritten-style font that Tadano liked to use for his handouts and thought, *What if this was Masaki's handwriting?* As a fan club member, I got Christmas and New Year's cards printed in his writing. What if I could cut them out and stitch them together to make a hand-lettered Masaki Ueno font? Maybe it would help me study. The idea took over my brain, and I started thinking about which letters might be missing from the cards, and what I'd actually need to do to make a font. Tadano's chalk stopped. The tip of it crumbled and sprinkles of white dust fell down the chalkboard. "Yes, your assignments were due today. Let's go ahead and collect them before we begin. I hope you all have them with you?" It sounded like a cicada had crawled into my ear. The noise rang out as though an uncountable number of eggs had been deposited inside my heavy head, and had just hatched. *I'm sure I wrote it down*, the me in my head protested. But there was no point writing it down if I was going to forget to review it afterward. "Come on up and hand them in," Tadano said, and while everybody else stood up, I stayed rooted to my chair. The boy in the seat in front of me got up nonchalantly, went up to Tadano's desk, and said, "I f'got. Sorryyy." The class tittered. I followed him up to the front of the room and said, "I forgot, sorry." No one laughed. I didn't act ingratiating enough to be "an airhead or a slacker."

Packing up to go home, I pulled a math textbook out of my desk. I flinched. Yu had told me she had Math fifth period, so I'd borrowed it from her saying I'd give it back at lunch. I went next door to her homeroom, but she was already gone.

< Sorry I forgot to return your textbook. I know you needed it for 5th. I'm really sorry. >

As I typed in the words, I knew I had no more excuses to offer. I turned the corner and saw the school nurse, who said, "Akari, don't forget to give me the report from your assessment." All the infirmary regulars got the first-name treatment. She always had her wavy hair in a thick ponytail that hung down the back of her white coat. It was too dazzling for summer and made my eyes flicker. I folded a sheet of loose-leaf into quarters and wrote down, in pen:

MATH TEXTBOOK
DOCTOR'S REPORT

After a second, I added:

GEO ASSIGNMENT

and then:

NARUMI UMBRELLA
FIELD TRIP MONEY
WRISTWATCH

I was standing in the middle of the hallway writing it down, holding the pen upright and pressing the tip of it into the loose-leaf, when a papery spasm hit my eyelids. The backpack I had tucked under my arm slid down to the floor. The light coming in through the hallway windows turned thicker, and the sun got low. The flesh of my cheek burned.

Hello again. It's been a while since I last posted, what with the news coming out, but I'm back. Just so you know, this article is only for followers, so please remember not to share it on any other platforms.

I think I'm right in saying the incident came as a shock, not only to us Masaki fans, but to everyone who follows Maza Maza. I never knew it until I saw it up close, but there really is nothing you can do about a fireball, is there? The blaze gets fanned from all directions, and just when you think they're starting to die down, someone tosses on more fuel, in the form of old tweets or photos, and sends the flames in a new direction. Stories spread about a falling-out between him and Akihito, of all things, when they've publicly acknowledged each other as soulmates. There was also an allegation that he bullied classmates at a high school in Himeji, his hometown. My oshi's school was a correspondence school in Tokyo that he rarely attended in person, so you almost have to hand it to some of the people who start rumors like these.

Many of you might be aware that a certain forum has been referring to the situation as a "dumpster fire." My oshi previously said in a TV appearance that he googles himself, because he thinks that even criticism can be grist for the mill. The thought of him seeing those words is intolerable, but what else can we do but sit tight and watch over him?

It's not much, but when I get to the next Maza Maza show my light stick will be Masaki blue. And in spite of the awful timing, when the next fan vote comes around, I don't want him to feel like we've deserted him. If you're a Masaki main, let's stay strong and stick together, now more than ever.

I was carsick. The deep-seated nausea inside my forehead and behind my eyeballs seemed impossible to uproot. "Can I open the window?" I said, but Mom said, "Don't," and for the first time I noticed the rain running down the outside of the glass.

"What were you writing?" my sister asked wearily from the seat beside me, rocked by the motion of the car.

"Blog post."

"Your oshi?"

I exhaled through my nose and said yes. My empty stomach spasmed.

"One I can read?"

"It's limited access. Followers only."

"Huh."

My sister sometimes had things to say about my fandom activity. "Why him?" she'd ask, curious. "I didn't know you were into the 'lightly salted' type. Akihito has stronger features, and Sena's a better singer, no?"

It was a stupid question. How could there be an answer? I liked him, so I came to like his singing, dancing, talk, personality, presence—everything about him. It was the reverse of that saying "Hate the monk, hate his robes." If you fell in love with the monk, even the frays in his robe became loveable. I thought that was pretty normal.

"So when are you gonna pay me back?" my sister said, sounding like it didn't much matter to her, and I said, "Oh, sorry," with the same energy. It was about some merch I'd bought online, cash on delivery. "Next time I get paid," I promised. "The fan vote's soon, so after that?"

"Huh," she said again. "How much do you think it'll affect his ranking?"

"Hard to say," I said. "I guess it depends on the proportion of casuals."

"Because they'll drift, you mean?"

"I think a lot of fans who joined after *SL* will leave."

My oshi's popularity had skyrocketed after his role in the romantic movie *Stainless Love*. He'd only had a supporting role as the heroine's younger brother figure, but had won over a lot of new fans with his unpolished and earnest portrayal, so it seemed likely that this incident would be especially damaging.

Mom suddenly pounded the steering wheel, sounding the horn. "Watch what you're doing," she said under her breath, complaining at the car in the opposing lane, which couldn't hear her.

My sister gulped as if she was the one in trouble. She'd always been like this. She'd prattle on about nothing while being tuned into Mom's mood the whole time. Mom went quiet whenever something got on her nerves, and my sister talked even more to make up for it.

I'd been told my grandma was the reason we didn't go with Dad years ago, when he was first posted overseas. According to her, it was ungrateful of us to leave her on her own as a widow, and so she made Mom and us stay behind. Mom never had a good word to say about her.

My sister rummaged around in the plastic bag from the hospital kiosk and cracked open a bottle of tea. She took a sip, checked the ingredients, and raised it to her lips again. With her mouth still full, she knit her brows and waved it at me, and then swallowed audibly and asked, "Want some?" "Oh, sure," I said, and took it from her, but the car's shaking made its mouth hit against my teeth and the tea nearly spill from my lips. The liquid poured into my empty stomach soothingly. It had been two years since my grandma had undergone a gastrostomy, but even though they'd explained how when people who became unable to swallow food, they opened a hole directly into their stomach and pumped in nutrition through a tube, the information had never really clicked. There was no food or drink allowed in the hospital room, so we always had to skip lunch when we visited in the middle of the day.

I felt too carsick to keep looking at a screen, so I put my earbuds in and listened to some music. The album had come out before the flame-up, and my oshi, who'd come out on top in the last fan vote, had a solo number, "Fork-Tongued Ondine," which he'd also written the lyrics for. It started with a distinctive guitar riff, and then, after a breath, the husky vocal came in on top. I sensed body heat across the back of my shoulders. Compared to the group's recent songs, which sounded more electronic, the song was pared down, with a melancholy vibe: *Sinking your crooked canine into the horizon* . . . When the song first came out, some fans who had romantic feelings toward my oshi had scoured the internet trying to find the woman with the crooked tooth.

I opened my eyes. Rain blurred the boundary between sky and water into a gray haze. The houses clinging to the shore looked hemmed in by the dark clouds. Coming into contact with my oshi's world changed what I saw. I looked at my reflection in the window, at the dry tongue inside its dark, warm-looking mouth, and silently mouthed the lyrics. It made me feel like my oshi's voice streaming into my ears was leaking out between my lips. His voice overlaid my voice, and his vision overlapped mine.

Mom turned the steering wheel. The drops of rain falling beyond the reach of the windshield wipers trailed down the window, and the glass—scrubbed clear by the beat of the wipers—clouded again. The rows of trees lost their outlines, leaving my eyes with only a vivid impression of green.

✳

The leaden weight of being carsick had left my body by the time we got home. "Miss Akari Yamashita, there's something here for you." My sister handed me a package of CDs, and I went to my room and carefully unwrapped them and took out the voting tokens. Each two-thousand yen CD came with one vote, so these meant I had fifteen votes. The results determined the number of lead vocals and center spots each member had on the next album, and the member with the most votes would get a long solo. Every batch of ten votes also got you a handshake with your chosen idol, so it was a sweet deal.

Akihito Saito • Masaki Ueno • Mifuyu Tachibana •
Mina Okano • Toru Sena

I scanned the serial number on each coupon and selected Masaki's name, displayed in blue. Once I finished entering the numbers for each of my ten coupons, I checked on my blog, but the view count was going up more slowly than usual. I remembered I'd set the post to followers only. Almost all the comments started with words of concern, like < How have you been? > and < We've missed you! >, and I realized that I'd been tweeting less since the whole flame-up. Taka, Komusō, Akihito's Duck (known as Duckie), Molasses Lozenge—I responded to each of them and then started writing to Caterpillar, my fellow Masaki fan, who as usual had written the longest comment. She changed her display name daily, from < Hungry Caterpillar > to < Caterpillar Anniversary > to < Caterpillar @ Feeling Bruised >. Currently her name was a row of bug and sweet potato emoji.

< Akariiii!! I've missed you! When you stopped updating it was like tumbleweeds around here so I went back into your old posts to get my fix, if that ran your hit counter up that was all me lol. Really feel this one!! You're exactly right I'm worried and unsure but we can't let rumors get us down, right? . . . Just so relieved to hear you say this Akari. Your writing is so mature, you're like our wise older sister or something? Anyway, looking forward to more updates soon! I know people are down on Masaki these days but seriously this right now is when we need to show up and represent, let's gooo! >

< Caterpillar thanks for your comment~~ Sorry to make you wait, but I'm happy you did haha. No way, I'm not mature or wise . . . Yeah, a lot to think about but we can do it! >

Caterpillar's words brimmed with charm and energy. We were different ages, went to different schools, and lived in different parts of the country; our love for Maza Maza was the only thing that connected us. But through all the comments and the grumbling Monday morning commutes and "Photo Friday Oshi Love-In" threads, and staying up into the night discussing this and that and how precious or incredible it was, I'd come to know my followers' lives through the screen and feel close to them. Just as they thought of me as a calm, dependable type, maybe they were each a little different than they seemed. But this world where I showed up with my half-made-up persona was a kinder place. We all cried out our love for our oshi, and that was a part of life.

< Gotta drag myself into the shower >

< You can do it, your oshi's waiting! >

< Omg no way I'm there >

< Went to my reunion and spammed my oshi's solos at karaoke~ >

< Wow respect! How did it go down? >

< Too awkward to pull it off and killed the vibe (>_<) >

< We salute you >

< Chin up! >

Oshis left suddenly, either through retirement, or by graduating from their groups, or in some scandal. There were musicians who'd gone missing or passed away without warning. When I pictured a world without my oshi, I thought about saying goodbye to the people here, too. It was our oshi that brought us together, and without him, we'd all go our separate ways. Some people moved over into different genres like Narumi had, but I knew I could never find another oshi. Masaki would always be my one and only. He alone moved me, spoke to me, accepted me.

✳

Each time the group released a new single, I displayed the CD on the shelf that in fandom circles was known as a "shrine." My room was a chaotic mess of dirty clothes, mystery bottles of soft drinks, textbooks opened and left facedown, and handouts tucked into things, but all the light and air that entered it was colored blue by the cerulean curtains and the azure glass lampshade. Idol groups generally assigned each member an official color, which would be used for the light sticks that fans would hold up to show your support at a performance or for other individual merch. My oshi's was blue, so I systematically surrounded myself with everything blue. Just being in a blue space made me feel calm.

The center of this room was obvious from the moment you stepped in. Like the cross inside a church, or the main deity in a temple, a big signed photo of my oshi was displayed on the highest shelf, and around it an array of posters and photos spread across the walls, framed in subtly different shades of cobalt, indigo, teal, and sky blue. The shelves were packed with DVDs, CDs, magazines, and flyers in chronological order, stacked up in layers like geological strata. Every release day, the CD on the highest shelf moved to the next one down to make way for the newest disc.

I couldn't manage life the way everyone else easily seemed

to, and I struggled with the messy consequences every day. But pushing my oshi was the center of my life, a given, and my one point of clarity. It was more than a core—it was my backbone.

I could see that normal people fleshed out their days with schoolwork, and activities, and part-time jobs that gave them money to go out with friends to the movies or to eat or buy clothes, which enriched their lives. I was moving in the opposite direction. My entire experience was increasingly concentrated into this backbone, as if I was going through some kind of ordeal to purify myself. Everything that was unnecessary fell away, until my spine was all that was left.

< Hi Akari >

< Reminder that I need your shift requests for over the summer vacation. >

I got a text from Miss Sachiyo, and still lying on the floor, I opened up my calendar app. My oshi work dictated my schedule, so I asked for an early finish on the day the fan vote results would be announced and obviously avoided the date of the meet and greet that would follow. I kept the day after free, too, so I could soak in the afterglow. But there were also CDs to buy and concerts to go to in the spring. I always ended up spending more than I thought, so I wanted to schedule in as many days of work as I could. Last year, when my oshi was in a play, I'd felt so inconsolable after each performance I attended that I wanted to see it again, and I'd find myself, yet again, returning to the "Future Tickets" counter. The show program was a must-buy, since it had cast interviews, and I'd already bought the original book that the play was adapted from (I wanted to watch the opening night without preconceptions, so I waited to read it afterward), but I wanted a copy of the edition with the tie-in cover that featured the stage set design on it, too. Having bought so much merch, when it came to photos, I thought I'd stick to getting just the ones I liked most, but once I saw the samples pinned up on the board I changed my mind. There were two shots each of my oshi in a kimono and dressed as an old-fashioned student, and one shot of him vomiting blood; after seeing them all I didn't feel like I could leave without the full set. Even if the same scene was contained in the DVD, from the same angle, the impact of that single moment lifted out of its surroundings could only be captured by a photograph. If I didn't get them while I could, I might never have another chance. I said, "All of them, please," and so did the woman after me. My living, moving oshi would be lost as soon as the show was over, but I wanted to take in every drop of what he was giving us, from the first look to the last breath. I wanted to remember that sensation of sitting alone in my seat feeling my chest fill up, to keep it with me, and I wanted the photos and the videos and the merch that would point me back to it. In his cast interview, he'd said, "Some people might think it's not my place as a pop artist to be in a play. I heard a lot of that online when it was first announced." But as an idol who was used to being in the limelight, his stage presence easily stood up to that of the real actors in the production. Most important, he was a natural match for the character, whose refusal to compromise on his principles became his downfall. His performance seemed to pass muster with the theater crowd, too.

I'd need all the money I could get for the tour, so in the end I requested a shift almost every day and sent in the list to Miss Sachiyo. *No school means no distractions . . . I can give my entire summer to my oshi.* The simplicity of that felt like my own, definite joy.

I woke to my oshi's voice and made my usual round of websites. I opened my blog and caught up on the comments and likes, and tapped on one to reread the original post.

Hello dear friends, how are you? My news is that I finally got one—yes, none other than the item officially known as the "Voiceful ★ Heartbeat Alarm Clock." I must admit I'm not sure where to start, from its frankly cringeworthy name to its design with the stylized minute and hour hands and my oshi's awkward smiling photo printed on the clock face. Ever since we saw the promo, people have been saying they'd have preferred something more understated—maybe a pen with a logo, or a pouch? Others have called it an idol merch triple threat—useless, embarrassing, and expensive—but funnily enough it seems like quite a few of us have gotten one anyway. For all our grumbling, we'll turn around and go buy an 8,800 yen alarm clock (!). We're easy marks, I know. But that's merch acquisition syndrome for you.

So this one was nearly a flop before it even went on sale, but do you know what? I actually really like it. Picture it—your oshi's voice being the first thing you hear every morning. "🎵 Ding-a-ling-a-ling 🎶 You know what time it is! Rise and shine! 🎵 Ding-a-ling-a-ling 🎶 You know what time it is! Rise and shine!" My foggy mind focuses instantly, and when I press down on the light-blue unit, it says, "You got this. Get out there and have a great day." Well, sign me up. Cheesy lines like this usually make me squirm, but when I picture oh-so-dignified Masaki recording these phrases, the idea is hilarious and extremely treasurable. He makes me breathe easier no matter how cold the day is. The heaviness melts out of my body, he warms me from my core and, honestly, gives me the strength to get through the day. My oshi relights the fire of life for me every morning. So, what with this and that, I'm still getting sucked dry by Maza Maza's management, but I love every minute of it.

The alarm clock review post, written before the blowup, was so casual I almost didn't recognize it, and I felt a little sheepish. Komusō, already—more like *still*—up, had posted a picture to her Insta story showing a platter of dried squid and cheese cod bites, a can of energy drink, and her oshi, Sena, on TV in the background, along with the caption:

< The planet: still round
Work: still endless
My oshi: still sacred >

Her posts were always along these lines, but as far as I could tell from her selfies, she had a pixie cut and was always groomed to the tips of her nails, and dressed from head to toe in high-fashion brands even I knew the names of. The official site's Updates box listed "Confirmation of BAKUON performance," and while the message touched on the incident from the other day, it confirmed that the concert would be going ahead as planned and that Masaki Ueno would appear. As expected, social media was awash with people criticizing the decision, but I was just glad that my first opportunity to see my oshi since the flame war hadn't been canceled. I sensed a new momentum in my body, and walking over the things scattered on the floor, I headed to the bathroom. The sensations of the zipper on a pair of jeans, the cover on a manga, and the saw-toothed edge of a bag of potato chips dug into the soles of my feet and climbed nearly up to my knees. My sister, who'd been pressing toner or something into her face with the palms of her hands, swatted away my hand as I reached for my toothbrush and said, "You know Mom got called into school?

"You should have told us earlier," she said.

She kept her left hand pressed to the surface of her face and opened a bottle of lotion with her right. Instead of answering, I stuck my toothbrush into my mouth. I washed my face, and without putting on any makeup, I gathered my hair up tightly enough to draw the ends of my eyes upward, which I hoped made me look a little more awake. I tugged a navy-blue polo shirt from its hanger, stretching out the neckline, and pulled it over my head. Stuffing a sky-blue lace handkerchief and a pair of glasses with ultramarine rims into my bag, I checked the day's horoscope. My oshi's sign, Leo, was ranked fourth for the day, and his lucky item was a pen, so I grabbed a ball-point with a blue rubber strap and shoved it into an inside pocket. I left without checking my own star sign. It wasn't important.

The restaurant I waitressed at was down the narrowest of the three streets leading away from the train station, going to the right. Groups of men working at the pachinko parlor or the apartments under construction behind it often came in for lunch, the hems of their pants caked in mud. Then, at the end of the day, they came back to drink. I was finally learning to recognize some of the regulars, but at night we got parties of office workers, whose gait and demeanor were often completely different when they left from when they came in. The sign outside said "Nakakko Canteen," but because we stayed open late and served alcohol, the place was more like an iza-kaya. When I went in after seeing the "Staff Wanted" flyer in the window, Miss Sachiyo had said, "We don't hire a lot of high schoolers." I found out they were having trouble finding staff when Kou, who was a college senior, quit as soon as I started, telling me, "I'm so glad you joined. Miss Sachiyo's been refusing to let me leave."

There were a lot of different threads to follow before we opened, starting with putting bubbles in the filtered water and refreshing the bottles of whiskey, getting the pork out of the freezer because we needed it every day, putting away the tableware that had been left to dry overnight, and sharpening the knives. I couldn't count the number of times Miss Sachiyo had told me off before the tasks had become muscle memory. I drilled the branching routes into my head—*when this happens then do that, if that happens it means this*—but when things got busy there was no more time to look at my notes, and then everything seemed to be an exception to the rules, and went tumbling out of my mind.

The smell of thick pork broth from the ramen place across the street came in with a gust of night air, and Chef and I called out, "Welcome!" Chef was slim and spoke in a soft tone, but when we greeted the customers his voice sounded as deep as the best of them. Katsu-san came in, opening the door with his fat fingers, and when I said Miss Sachiyo had gone to get something from the stockroom out back, he told me to give him an extra splash of whiskey. Katsu-san had a square-set face; the one with the narrow chin and eyes was Higashi-san; the one in the undershirt, who was young and smiley but had a cold gleam in the whites of his eyes, I couldn't remember. I served the three regulars with hot hand towels and edamame, laid down their chopsticks and an ashtray, and then before I could get my notepad out, I heard, "A highball, on the strong side. What, that costs more? How about just a little splash?" And just like that, the sequence recorded in my body came to a stop.

"Give her a break," Higashi-san said, lifting the towel draped over the back of his neck.

"Nah," Katsu-san said. "Come on, give me just a little extra," he said, and closed one eye at me, so I asked him to wait a minute, and then the woman sitting nearest the aisle in the group I'd showed to a private room earlier leaned back and said, "Um, I've spilled my drink?" so I wrote down "Table 3" and said, "I'll be with you right away." I found the staff price list that was kept under the cash register, which said:

Highball———¥400
Highball (strong)———¥520
Highball (stein)———¥540
Highball (stein, strong)———¥610

As soon as I showed it to Katsu-san, he looked bored and said, "Fine, three beers, then," without even checking with the others.

Akari, dear, you need to remember. It's the smile. No matter what, you need to smile. That's what hospitality is all about. I pictured Miss Sachiyo's face reflected in the square mirror spattered with the residue of droplets, looking serious with her mouth open, meticulously applying thick, dark lipstick all the way to the edges of her lips, and realized, *I messed up.* I made my way back to the kitchen. Chef—who had lost so much weight recently that I thought he must be sick or something—called my name and smiled at me, and I realized that he'd gotten a bowl for the edamame shells off the shelf for me. I thanked him and took it to the counter, where Higashi-san looked at me and said, "Hey, Little Akari's back." He'd called me Little Akari since the day I tripped and fell carrying three mugs of beer in my hands. After several rounds of coming back to their table to take care of tasks I should have done already, he said, "Little Akari's about to cry," and I said "Sorry," which was greeted by calls from other tables saying "Um, sorry"—"Excuse me"—and I remembered how I'd been instructed to stay calm and ask for help as soon as things got busy, because that led to mistakes, which was bad customer service, so I went to try and get Miss Sachiyo from the storeroom out back, but then on my way there the same woman said, a bit stiffly, "I'm sorry, but I told you I spilled a drink."

"I'm sorry, I'll clean it up."

"No, that's fine, can we just get some towels? If it isn't too much trouble."

"Akari, don't worry, I'll take care of it. You get the beers," Chef said, and he put the pork back in the refrigerator. I understood what it meant for him to leave the kitchen, but anxiety streamed into my thoughts and turned them cloudy like milk. A group of men, who'd been the picture of decorum when they came in, yelled for the check, but their voices only got as far as my ears, and I headed onto the floor again, urged forward by the faint fizz coming from the tops of the three beers on my tray.

"There she is," Katsu-san said, his lip curling slightly. He turned to me with the same expression and said, "You get paid for this, don't you? You should start taking it seriously." It felt like he'd taken my gaze, which must have been swimming in midair, and nailed it firmly back into my eyeballs.

"So, to order," he said, suddenly cheerful again. "Let's have ginger pork, yellowtail daikon, stewed beef tendon, the fried chicken, and squid, too . . ."

As I noted these down using abbreviations, I heard Chef, who'd finished ringing up the party's check, and Miss Sachiyo, who'd come back from the storeroom, both call out, "See you again!" and I joined them, my voice bursting from my choked throat. The wind was howling. I heard the rattle of the door closing, the voices coming through the wavy glass talking about moving on to the next bar, the hard sound of the stream of water hitting the sink as Miss Sachiyo rinsed and propped up the plates, the noises of the extractor fan and the refrigerator, Chef's soft voice saying, "Calm down, Akari. Everything's going to be okay, just calm down." I said, "Yes, I know, I'm sorry," but what did it mean to calm down? When I hurried I just made mistakes, and when I tried to stop it was like a fuse tripped— even as I thought about all this, my conscious mind protested that there were still more customers waiting for attention, and my racing thoughts piled up inside me until they overflowed and started backing up. I was about to choke on the "Sorrys" surrounding me, not knowing whether they were from me or the customers. I stole a glance at the clock on the wall near the seam where one piece of yellowed wallpaper curled away from another. An hour of work paid for a photo, two hours was a CD, and when I earned ten thousand yen that was a ticket to a live event. I was paying the price for just trying to get through work doing the bare minimum. I could see the wrinkles carving themselves into Chef's face as he wiped down a table with a self-conscious smile.

*

Carrying two stacked plastic crates full of bottles, I pushed the back door open with my shoulder and felt the air breeze past my neck, still warm from the heat of the day, and briefly drive away the rising smells of grass and the neighborhood cats' urine. I held my breath and propelled my body through the doorway and, with it, the crates with the rattling bottles inside them. "Hey," someone said, and looking up from my half-crouch, I saw the three men who'd just left. They'd gone on to order a bottle of potato shochu, and even in the dark I could see that Katsu-san's face was ruddy and bloated. Miss Sachiyo had discreetly told me his full name so I could mark it on the bottle they'd put behind the bar.

Mr. Katsumoto
July 30

"Where're you going? Over here?"

My body suddenly got lighter, or, more accurately, got lifted up, and a gush of sweat erupted inside the T-shirt I was wearing under my apron.

"Katsu-san, no, please, you can't—"

"Easy peasy." His voice clouded with effort as he said, "Lift anything, just gotta put your back into it," and his legs seemed to twist around, and the other man in the tank top quickly stepped in to support the weight of both him and the crates.

"These things are pretty heavy to carry, for a girl," he said, and I noticed he was drunk, too. He must be one of those people whose words came out easier once they were lubricated by some alcohol. I dipped my head and said, "Thank you," and I put the crates he'd handed off to me down by the wall. As I was about to go back inside with a fresh crate of full bottles from the open storeroom, Miss Sachiyo came out carrying a trash can, and Higashi-san, who didn't seem drunk at all, said to her, "She works hard for a student. What do they spend it on these days?"

"There's a pop idol she follows. Isn't that right?" Miss Sachiyo said, propping the back door open with a crate of empty cans.

"An idol? Really?" the man in the tank top said, loudly.

"You know what girls are like. They get their hearts set on a pretty face."

"At least she's still young. But she should get to know some real men. Before she misses the boat."

As Miss Sachiyo and Katsu-san talked behind me I remembered that empty cans needed to be thrown out, so I started taking them out of the crate and putting them in the trash can. The back door pushed the emptying crate aside and began to swing closed.

"Little Akari here's just trying to get it right. Aren't you?" Higashi-san said suddenly. He'd been watching me with his arms crossed over his chest.

"That's it," Katsu-san said. "You ask for a little extra splash, but she won't do it. Come on! All the other girls said yes."

"All right, Katsu-san," Miss Sachiyo said. She was smiling.

✳

People never thought I was trying to do things right. They usually just said I was lazy.

Going back, it all started with the kanji for the number "four." The kanji for "one," "two," and "three" looked like this:

$$一, 二, 三$$

Simple. But then why did "four" look like this?

四

Not to mention how 一, 二, and 三 each had the same number of strokes as the number they represented, while "four" needed *five* strokes (and "five" only had four). "Practice makes perfect," my teacher used to say, but no matter how many times I copied out the characters for the numbers one to ten, mine never turned out like the other kids'.

Mom also used to quiz my older sister, Hikari, and me on our multiplication tables or our ABCs at bath time. She'd make us stay in the water until we'd recited them correctly. Except I never could. I could never get the letters and numbers to match up with the sounds my sister was making, and when my mind started to go blank Mom would say, "That's enough," and bundle me out of the water. Hikari, wrapped in a towel with a cartoon character's face on it, having earned her right to get out and dry off, usually watched me in silence, but one day she complained.

"It's not fair! How come Akari can get out when she hasn't even said it right? Why'm I the only one that has to?"

I didn't remember what Mom said to her. I was still slithering around in the lukewarm water, flushed and unable to get purchase on the side of the tub that Hikari had climbed out of triumphantly. The metal chain attached to the plug in the drain hurt where it scraped against the skin of my belly; my body felt heavy as Mom pulled me out, and I didn't understand why my sister was jealous.

"Why do you only hug Akari?" Hikari said. From the way Mom's arms felt, I didn't think there was much of a hug to her embrace. She was just hauling something heavy. From my point of view, I'd much rather have been Hikari, able to answer the questions easily, get out first, and win Mom's approval.

It was the same with the kanji test at school. You had to keep taking it until you were able to write all the characters correctly, and Kotaro the booger-muncher and I were the last ones left. I practiced them in my workbook, filling in square after square. "That's how you learn your kanji," they said, so I wrote pages and pages until the knuckle at the base of my little finger turned completely black. The pages I'd covered in writing glinted in the light, but even though I felt lightheaded from the smell of pencil lead, I told myself I had to practice the characters until I filled up the whole notebook.

So I kept on writing the word "pasture," which I'd missed last time:

放牧 放牧
放牧 放牧
放牧 放牧

I wrote the word "possess":

所持 所持
所持 所持
所持 所持

and the word "to feel":

感じる 感じる
感じる 感じる
感じる 感じる

I thought I had them all memorized perfectly. I got "pasture" the right way around, unlike last time when I'd switched the two characters and written 牧放 instead of 放牧. I remembered the first character in "possess" but simplified half of the second one and ended up writing "place-waiting" instead. And I couldn't think of the upper half of the character for "to feel" and wrote just the lower half, which made "to heart." I messed up a few kanji I'd gotten correct the previous time, and in the end my score improved by just one point out of fifty. Even Kotaro overtook me, and by the end of the year I was the only one in the class who'd failed to pass the test.

Mom started putting a lot of energy into teaching Hikari and me, especially English. I didn't know how closely that was related to my father's posting abroad. By the time Mom was coaching us late into the night, as though to distract herself from her own insomnia, I was starting to learn to distance myself from studying in inconspicuous ways. Hikari said, "Mom, the problem is you never praise her," and took my side, telling me, "Hikki will teach you English." The only thing I still remembered from what my sister taught me was the "s" for third person singular. She lavished me with praise every time I added "s" to the end of a verb and went over it patiently when I forgot, so I focused all my attention on making sure each verb had an "s" on it before handing her my answers to check, and I got every question correct. Hikari was as proud of my success as if it was her own. But the next day, when she gave me a fresh list of verbs, the third person singular had slipped my mind entirely. I didn't do it on purpose. Hikari did her best to be tactful even as I could see the disappointment ooze out of her.

My sister was studying for her university entrance exams by the time she finally snapped. I was eating the stew Mom had made for dinner while she nagged at me through the door to the changing room. My sister had her books open and a small bowl of stew on the edge of the table. As usual, Mom was getting on my case about not studying.

I raised my voice toward the changing room and said, "I'm working hard! I'm trying!"

My sister, who had been studying, paused.

"Can you not?" she said. "It drives me crazy when you do that. It's insulting. I'm up late studying every night. And Mom goes to work even though she can't sleep and she feels nauseous and has a headache every morning. How is that remotely the same as you spending all your time chasing after some idol? Where do you find the nerve to say you're trying?"

"Can't we just be trying in our own ways?"

My sister watched me lift a piece of daikon with my chopsticks and put it in my mouth. She burst out crying.

"No," she said. Tears fell on her notebook. Her handwriting was small and easily legible even in her class notes. "You don't need to do it. You don't need to try. Just stop *pretending* you're trying. It's not the same."

The piece of daikon fell back into the dish with a brothy splat. I wiped at the tabletop with a tissue. Hikari, lashing out, said, "Clean it properly," and deliberately moved her books away.

I'm trying to clean it, I thought, *and anyway I never said it was the same.* I tried to tell her, but she kept crying and tangling up the thread of what I needed to say.

It didn't make any sense. I couldn't tell when she'd defend me, and when she'd get mad. My sister expressed herself not through logic, but through her body, which spoke and cried and angered.

Mom didn't get angry so much as judge. She would make snap decisions. My sister would pick up on them immediately and wear herself down trying to keep the peace.

Once, I overheard Mom talking about me. I'd woken up around three a.m. and gotten out of bed to go to the bathroom. I saw light leaking out from under the door to the living room. I could hear voices. My sister was probably plucking Mom's gray hairs again.

"Ow. That wasn't a gray, I felt it."

"It was streaky."

In my half-asleep state, the warm light appeared as an indistinct glow.

Without meaning to, I was listening for Mom's voice behind the door. I heard her say something and apologize.

"I'm sorry about Akari. I know it's hard for you."

My toenails were long. Hair was sprouting from my big toe, which I thought I'd shaved. Why did things continue to grow out of me no matter how much I cut and plucked? It felt intolerable.

"I know," I heard Hikari say quietly. "But she can't do anything."

I stepped into the living room. Its brightness made the dim hallway seem like a dream, and I could suddenly see the shapes of the TV, Mom's houseplants, and the cups on the coffee table with great clarity. My sister didn't look up. Mom, almost defiantly, said, "Take your laundry with you."

I ignored her. I strode forward and took a tissue, and got the nail clippers from the bottom drawer of the dresser. I clipped my nails. The sound rang out. My toenails were square and hard to clip without catching skin. Mom said something. I dug the end of the clippers under the nail where it was embedded in the flesh of my toe and squeezed. A sliver of nail went flying. When I was done, my attention moved to the hairs growing from my toes, and I realized that the tweezers were already out.

"Can I?" I said to my sister. Before she could say anything, I took the small silver tweezers out of her hand and started plucking, ignoring Mom trying to interject. I saw the drops of fluid on the ends of the short dark hairs, and felt ashamed. I couldn't understand why I had to keep being confronted, endlessly, with what kept growing and growing no matter how much I cut and plucked. Why I always had to feel this way about everything.

It was around then that I found my oshi again. I'd somehow made it into high school while grinding away at a life that was three steps forward and two steps back. My oshi was radiant. It was a radiance born of pushing himself continually for twenty years, ever since he was first thrown in front of the camera as a child. "When I started out, I was surrounded by adults I had to please, and for a while I thought the industry was just something I'd been forced into, but the first time I performed as an idol—I would have been eighteen—and I saw the silver streamers shooting upward from the stage, and heard the crowd noise fill up the venue until it seemed like it was going to burst, my mind suddenly turned quiet, and I thought: You know what? I'm here, and I'm going to give you something to scream about." I think this moment, which he spoke about once, was the moment he started to give off a light of his own.

He shone, but he was also human. He spoke in decisive statements that invited misunderstanding. He often kept his lips in a social curve, but when he was really happy, he smiled as though he was trying to keep his smile hidden on the inside of his face. He sounded confident on talk shows, but on variety shows he seemed uncertain, and you could see his gaze wavering. He seemed to have found a taste for being the "useless" one of the group since one InstaLive when he had tried to take a sip of water from a plastic bottle with its cap screwed shut. His selfies were unflattering (although his face was good enough for this to be forgivable), but he was good at taking pictures of other things. Everything about him was precious. When it came to my oshi, I wanted to offer him everything I had. "I'll give you everything" sounds like a line from a cheap romance drama, but his existence and my witnessing of it were all I asked for, so when Katsu-san or Miss Sachiyo talked about "getting to know some actual men," I didn't know what they meant.

There were so many ways of being in the world—friends, acquaintances, boyfriends and girlfriends, family—all of which involved influencing each other and adjusting daily in subtle ways. People who wanted balanced, reciprocal relationships said there was something unhealthy about connections that were only one-way. *Stop pining over him, you don't have a chance. Why are you always the one making sacrifices for her?* It was tiresome being told I was being taken advantage of, when I had no expectation of getting anything in return. My devotion to my oshi was its own reward, and that worked well for me, so I just needed people to shut up about it. I wasn't looking for my oshi to return my feelings. Probably because I didn't even want to be seen or accepted the way I was now. I didn't know whether he'd feel positively about me if we ever met, and I didn't even think I'd choose to be by his side 24/7 if it were an option— even though, admittedly, exchanging a few words at a meet and greet would get me so excited I thought I might explode.

Phones and TV screens had a kind of grace built into their separation, like the distance between the stage and the audience. It was reassuring to sense someone's presence at a certain remove, so that the space couldn't be destroyed by interacting directly, or the relationship ruined by anything I did. More important, when I pushed my oshi, when I put all of myself on the line and went deep, the commitment might have been one-sided, but I felt more complete than I ever had before.

I copied out my oshi's basic stats onto loose-leaf paper in orange ink and quizzed myself on them using a sheet of clear red plastic.

> *Birth date: August 15, 1992*
> *Sun sign: Leo*
> *Blood type: B*
> *Hometown: Hyogo Prefecture*
> *Siblings: One sister (four years older)*
> *Favorite color: Blue*
> *— Joined Starlight Productions at age of three*
>   *months.*
> *— Mother and sister left the family around the*
>   *time he finished middle school.*
> *— Lived with his father (office worker),*
>   *grandfather, and grandmother.*
> *— Started a blog named "Masaki Ueno's blog"*
>   *but stopped updating after a year and a half.*
>   *Currently mainly active on Instagram. Twitter*

is announcements only.
— *Fan club was founded when he was sixteen.*
— *After numerous stage appearances, transferred*
from Starlight Productions to the Wonder
Agency at the age of eighteen, and debuted as a
member of the coed idol group Maza Maza.

I researched the background on plays that he was in, by drawing maps and character relationship diagrams, so I became pretty expert on Russian history and even got a good grade on a school test. When I blogged, the device came up with the right kanji for me, so I never had to worry about the awkwardness of the times we'd read one another's essays in class and people would point out all the words I'd gotten wrong.

To follow my oshi with my entire body and soul; to interpret him and record it on my blog. As I rewound the TV recording and took notes, I remembered how Hikari had once turned the same focus on her studies. My oshi had shown me there was something I could dedicate myself to. Today, my shift finished at three p.m., so there was a little less tiredness in my hair than usual as it waved in the wind on my way home. I got some ice water and sat cross-legged on the floor, and when I pressed the cloudy button into the grimy remote control, an image appeared on the flat screen, even less visible in the daylight. The fan vote results would be announced at four p.m., so I still had time. I checked my phone and saw that multiple Maza Maza keywords were trending online.

The sound of a recycling truck passed by the window. A small dog yapped at something. I peeled my thighs off the laminate, and the bones of my pelvis ached dully, and the air-conditioned floor felt more unyielding than usual. Four p.m. came, and the program started. I heard a key turn, and Mom came in from work.

"Akari," she said, sharply. "Leaving the window open with the air conditioner on? Are you listening to me?"

"You haven't even changed—I need to start the laundry," she said, and I said, "Okay. Okay." I got up with my eyes still glued to the TV, and swaying unsteadily, I got out of my jeans. "Draw the curtains, please," Mom said again. Suddenly, the screen went dark with a *bzzt*. For the first time, I looked my mom in the face. There was a stray strand of hair hanging down by her cheek.

"Are you listening?" She drew back the arm holding the remote control.

"Yeah, sorry, but it's important."

"You can't have it back."

"Why, though?"

"I've had enough."

I apologized as I was told to, closed the window as I was told to, and changed out of my work clothes into my pajamas as I was told to. I scrubbed the bathtub, washed the dishes left from when I'd microwaved a pouch of fried rice that morning, took the laundry my sister had folded earlier to my room, and got the remote control back, but by then the result had already been announced.

As soon as I saw my oshi in the fifth-place seat, I understood he'd come in last.

The inside of my head flashed a dark, red, confusing color, like anger. "What the hell?" I said, throwing the words against the inside of my mouth, and immediately they gained speed, generated heat. Last time, he'd been in center position, sitting on a throne draped in soft-looking fabric, smiling like he was embarrassed by the magnificent crown. His expression when he let down his guard was rare and adorable. I'd made it my wallpaper and replayed it often, and posted < **Precious, beloved, good job** >, but now that he sat perched on a common chair, one leg in front of the other, reacting to what the emcee was saying, I could barely look at his face. I couldn't bear it. Every fan sat along with their oshi in the chair their oshi was allocated.

< No, why? >
< This hurts. >

I typed quickly into my phone. As far as I could tell, I got a Like from everybody who was there refreshing in real time. Caterpillar reacted with a crying face emoji.

We can't compete, I thought. I realized how much damage the incident had done to my oshi. It had robbed him of something huge. I think all of us had bought at least double what we used to, but it wasn't about us fans trying harder. That being said, it was a narrow gap, less than a hundred votes, between him and Mina in fourth place. I'd used up nearly all of my paychecks buying fifty CDs, but still, I wondered, *What if I'd really pushed myself to the limit and bought a few more, maybe then* . . . If all of us had been able to buy a few more, he might have been spared quite so obvious a fall, from first to dead last. Previously, on a radio program, he'd expressed that the system wasn't very generous, and that while he was grateful for his fans' votes, he urged them not to overextend themselves. I knew he didn't care that much about the ranking. Still, I thought I could sense his discomfiture through the screen. "One last word from each of you," the emcee said, and my oshi, who was passed the mic first, took it and cradled it in his hands.

"The most important thing," he said, breathing out noisily, "is that after everything that happened, you still gave me 13,627 of your votes. I'm grateful. This wasn't what you hoped for. I'm sorry to fall short of your expectations, but I have no regrets. I'm feeling the weight of each and every vote. Thanks, everyone."

My oshi sometimes came under criticism for his extremely short comments, but this was enough for me. The curtains swayed, and on the flatscreen, it looked as though he was narrowing his eyes against the glare, too. The way he closed his eyes and wrinkled his nose was so endearing, I felt as though I was being wrung out from the depths of my chest.

When an athlete lost their last playoff game in their final year of high school, people said that was the end of their summer. But I felt like that day was when my real summer started.

I had to go all in. I vowed to have eyes only for my oshi. It was hard seeing my oshi's merch on the secondhand market, so I tried to give a good home to as many of the items as I could. I opened packages from Okayama and Okinawa, carefully dusted the old badges and photos, and made space for them on my shelves. I stopped spending money on anything other than oshi work. My job at the restaurant was still grueling, but when I thought I was doing it for my oshi, it was more than worth it.

On August 15, I bought a deep-yellow sponge cake from the best bakery I knew, lit candles around the chocolate plaque with my oshi's face drawn on it, posted it on my Insta story, and ate the whole thing. I started to struggle partway through, but I felt that to give up now would be to betray both my oshi and the cake, so I used the moisture of the strawberries to push down the whipped cream sticking in my throat. After forcing an entire cake into my shrunken stomach, I felt nauseated by the sugar rush and threw up. I went to the bathroom and stimulated the back of my tongue with two fingers, and my throat opened and the smell of what I had vomited ran up ahead of the taste, from my throat to my brow. The edges of my eyelids tightened, and tears seeped out. The sound of air crawling out of my body was immediately followed by a chunky flow of sweet-tasting vomit. A few drops of water splashed back from the bowl onto my cheek. I wiped my dirty fingers on a piece of toilet paper and flushed. As I kept going, the void in my abdomen twisted and twinged in pain. Scrubbing my hands under the water, I looked in the mirror and saw a woman with bloodshot eyes. Keeping eye contact with her, vacantly, I rinsed out my mouth, and saw a small amount of blood and stomach acid mixed in with the water as it swirled down the drain. It smelled. As my legs mounted the stairs and my arm reached for the handrail, at some point it became a struggle just to make it back to my room, and I wondered if this feeling was what I was really looking for.

I started to notice myself yearning to push my body to its limit, whittle it down, seek out hardship. Letting go of everything I had—time, money, energy—in service of something outside of myself. Almost as though by doing that, I could cleanse myself. That by pouring myself into it, and taking the pain in return, I could find some kind of value in my existence. I published on my blog every day, even though I didn't always have much to say. Overall views went up, but fewer people were reading each post. Checking social media got to be exhausting, so I logged out of the app. It wasn't views or likes I needed. What I needed was to keep pushing my oshi to the best of my ability.

Time stopped in the infirmary. From the cool white bed, the sound of the bell and the hallway noise it set off, and the rustling of leaves outside all seemed to recede into the distance. I shifted my gaze away from the fine pattern of white and gray on the ceiling. My vision focused on the glint of the chrome curtain rail, and then blurred again. My head was foggy, perhaps because I'd lost a lot of weight over the summer, and having started the new term while my rhythm was still thrown off, I couldn't keep up. Red spots like clumps of blood showed up on the right-hand edge of my field of view, and zits erupted all over my face. Mom said the zits were disgusting. Online advice said to wash gently and moisturize, but I didn't have time for that. Instead, I washed my face multiple times a day and grew out my hair to hide my face. It felt like a permanent version of the dizziness I got after staying too long in the bath, and I hadn't finished my homework and I'd forgotten my Classics handout, and my ears hurt from my earbuds because I had to listen to my oshi's a cappella lullaby all night to get some sleep. I spent most of my classes facedown on my desk, but in fourth-period English I had to get up for a group translation activity. The classroom was gloomy from the rain clouds hanging overhead, and maybe I imagined it, but no one seemed to be saying much. Still looking down, I picked my desk up and started moving. Clusters formed naturally and then readjusted, and at the end I was the only one left standing, elbows extended, desk hanging off my arms. My skin gathered heat, and I thought of the lines of sight tangling around every motion I made to look at the faces surrounding me and froze. The seconds ticking past added up inside my rib cage.

My body looped back and replayed that feeling from just a few hours earlier, and I curled into myself. I was on the verge of dissolving into sleep when the nurse moved the curtain slightly and said, "Hi, Akari? Mr. Arishima wants to have a word." I sat up. My guts, which had shifted while I'd lain on my side, lurched uncertainly. My homeroom teacher was waiting in the back. In the infirmary, all the teachers seemed different from when they were in the classroom or the teachers' room.

"What's the matter, Akari?" he said, sounding teasing, or bemused. He was probably in his late thirties and hardly moved his mouth when he talked. His voice was quiet for the classroom but fitting for the infirmary. I followed him into the student consultation room at the back, which was there to protect students' privacy. We'd barely sat down when he said, "I'm hearing from a lot of teachers you've been missing class."

"I'm sorry."

"Tired?"

"Yeah."

"What from?"

"Um, just because."

He raised his eyebrows deliberately, making an expression that said, *Oh dear*.

"It's none of my business, but you'll need to repeat the year if you go on like this. As I'm sure you know."

We talked through how I'd quit school if they held me back and what I'd do if I did—similar to conversations I'd already had at home. Then he said, "You're struggling with schoolwork?"

"I mean, I can't do it."

"Why do you think that is?"

I felt like something was crushing my throat. *Why can't I do it?* That was what I wanted to know. Tears swelled against my eyeballs, but before they brimmed over, I thought how ugly it would be to spill them over all my zits and held back. Perhaps Hikari wouldn't think twice about crying in a situation like this, but I found it needy and abject. It would be losing to my body. I pried my jaws away from each other. I relaxed my temples and shifted my awareness away, gradually. The wind was blowing. The air in the consultation room was thin, and I felt pressured. Instead of scolding me head-on, Mr. Arishima was resorting to persuasion.

"I still think you should graduate. You can keep pushing just a little longer. Think about your future."

I felt like what he was saying was true, but the voice in my head overwrote it with *But my present is already too much.* I was losing sight of the line between what I needed to accept and what I could run from in order to protect myself.

✳

I found out I'd failed junior year a month before graduation. After the meeting, Mom and I walked back to the train station together. I felt the same way I did when I went to the infirmary or went home early—like time had been ripped off and was suspended in midair—except even more strongly, and the feeling seemed to have infected her, too. Although we hadn't cried, we both looked tearstained as we walked. Things felt bizarre.

We'd decided I would quit, since repeating the year probably wouldn't make any difference.

I used to listen to my oshi's songs on the way to school every morning. I'd walk along to a slow ballad on days I had time, newer up-tempo songs when I was in a rush. The pace of the music totally changed how long it took to get to the station. His music controlled my stride, the rhythm of my legs.

Controlling myself took energy. It was much easier to ride the music and let it move me along, like a train or an escalator. On the way home, I sometimes noticed the people sitting on the train looking serene and carefree. I think it was because they were safe in the knowledge they were going somewhere. The relief of knowing they were moving forward, even though they weren't propelling themselves, gave them permission to feel safe being on their phones or dozing off. Waiting rooms, too. In a room where even the sunlight was cold, bundled up in your coat, just knowing there was something you were waiting for could bring a warm sense of relief. At home on your own couch, under a blanket soaked in your own odor and body heat, black anxiety built up for every moment you spent gaming or napping as the sun moved through the sky. Sometimes it was harder to be doing nothing than it was to do something.

My sister learned I'd quit school from the family group chat. She replied,

< OK. That must have been hard. You did your best. >

Later that day, she barged into my room and said, "Hey. I know you probably feel bad. But take a break for a while."

She looked around my blue room uncomfortably. Mom came in all the time, but I wondered how long it had been since my sister had visited from her room next to mine.

"Yeah. Thanks."

"Okay," she said. Her intonation was ambiguous, neither a question nor a statement.

I said, "Yeah."

The person who was least able to accept that I had dropped out was Mom. Everything in her life right now was falling short of what she envisioned. Not only was her younger daughter a dropout, but her elderly mother's health was failing, and her new doctor was unfriendly. Her direct report was pregnant, leaving her with more work to do. The electricity bill was going up. The plants the couple next door had planted were growing onto our property. Dad's company had postponed his visit home. The handle fell off her new frying pan, and the manufacturer's replacement hadn't arrived even though she'd called them a week ago.

Her insomnia seemed to be getting worse by the day. She said she was getting more gray hairs and spent time examining her head in the mirror, searching them out. Her dark circles got darker. My sister made her furious by buying her a concealer that was getting rave reviews for hiding undereye discoloration. My sister cried. Her cries were piercing and made Mom even angrier.

Sighs settled over the living room, and sobs soaked into the gaps between the floorboards and into the wood grain of the wardrobes. Maybe that was how a home broke down over the years, as the sound of doors slamming and chairs roughly scraping the floor built up like dust, and the slow drip of gnashing teeth and resentful grumbling bloomed into mildew. Our teetering, half-defunct household almost seemed to be asking to collapse. Then we got the news that Grandma had died.

I came home from work after getting shouted at for a grilled saury that was cold by the time I could serve it to find Mom combing her hair and locking up.

"We're leaving *now*," she said. "Grandma died."

Mom stabbed at the remote control and shut off the TV. The fluorescent lights and the ventilation switched off, leaving only silence, and my sister, already red-eyed, refilled plastic bottles with water.

"Go get changed."

The news came out of nowhere. It was like we'd been making our way through a grab bag of individually wrapped chocolates and had suddenly been told we'd just eaten the last one.

In the car, nobody said anything for a while. Only Mom was

crying, though she was calm and driving. Her expression was tense, and the tears just rolled down her face. She wiped them mechanically, as though to say they were getting in the way of her seeing the road. When we reached the highway, my sister turned her back to me to watch the lights speeding past in streaks of color. A notification came in—Narumi asking if we could talk tonight. From Narumi's words, I pictured her face before she got plastic surgery. She'd gotten double eyelids in the winter break just before I left school. Her eyes were still swollen when we came back. The students gossiped about it kind of halfheartedly, but none of it registered in her eyes, which opened wider with each day that went on. She had eyes only for her oshi. I replied < OK! > with a Maza Maza voice sticker. I pressed "send," and from my phone, Sena's cheery voice called out "Okay!" My sister shifted slightly but kept looking out the window.

✳

While Mom went to accompany my grandmother's body back from the hospital, Hikari and I arrived at the house where Mom had grown up. My sister moved the newspapers and containers of old seaweed and pickled plums off to the side of the table and moistened a dry, stiff cloth. A swipe of the dusty table revealed the brighter color underneath. On the surface, which reflected the round shape of the fluorescent light above our heads, we spread out the bento boxes we'd bought at a no-name convenience store and laid out the disposable chopsticks. The fried chicken and the katsu looked bigger than the ones sold at our local store. I said, "Do you wanna eat?" and she said, "Not really. But you go ahead," and looked at the clock.

I found a pair of sandals by the veranda and went out into the garden. There was a stone wall and a pond imprecisely reflecting the moon. I called Narumi, who picked up on the first ring.

"Yoo-hoo!"

The sound of her voice still brought up her old face.

"How's it going?" I asked.

"Been a while!" she said.

"Yeah."

"Miss seeing you on the train."

"I've been dealing with some stuff."

"I hear ya."

"Yeah."

There was a short silence.

"But what's your news?" I said.

"Is it obvious? Heads up, it's kind of a major development."

I'd been teetering on the rocks outlining the pond as we talked, balancing front to back on the soles of my sneakers, but I came back down to ground.

"What is it? Tell me tell me."

"We connected."

"*Wooow*," I said. A small flying insect touched my open lips, and I hurriedly swatted it away. I started to feel dizzy, so I sat down heavily on the veranda.

"It really happened, wow, I'm happy for you."

"It's the double lid effect."

"No way that did it."

"No, for real."

She sounded like she meant it. I could even picture her making her 100 *percent serious* face.

"He's really into big, wide eyes with parallel folds. He acts different since I got them. He even said so on our date."

"Hold up, are you dating?"

"Well, it's like—not exactly but . . . ?"

Still in my sandals, I rolled onto my back, and with the momentum of it I exhaled and said, "Wow. You're kidding. For real? Huh . . ." Now I was the one with the emoji-like expression of surprise pointed at the ceiling. Maybe if I kept putting out uncomplicated emotions, I could eventually turn into an uncomplicated person. We talked about easy things for a while and then hung up.

The smell of the night sea drifted over to me. The water was just behind the mossy stone wall. I imagined the oily sea ringing portentously. I felt something dangerous and destabilizing rear up from somewhere deep inside my awareness. I remembered when my grandpa died, how Grandma had been, and the memory was swallowed up immediately into the darkness of the sea. I pictured her last moments, and then that, too, was blotted out by the water.

Trying to escape the terror, I returned to the living room. Mom was back, and Dad, who'd gotten leave from his posting, arrived, too. We were all staying in my grandmother's house until the funeral.

I unlocked my phone. I watched old vids that were available for free, set the quality to "highest," and took screenshots. I downloaded fan club–exclusive candids. My oshi was invariably adorable. It was a different kind of adorable from the color pink, or lovely ribbons and frills. It wasn't just about his looks, either. It was more like the dedication of the crow with seven chicks, in the nursery rhyme. It was a protective kind of love that made your heart ache and was stronger than anything, and I couldn't imagine it changing in the future no matter what he did, or what happened.

"Is there a hair dryer around here?" my sister asked the room, patting her hair with the faded towel draped around her neck.

Mom took a breath and said, "Yeah, maybe," and turned toward the variety show still playing on the TV.

"Akari, why don't you go next," Dad said.

"What about you?"

"I'll wait."

"Get going," Mom said. "You're slow enough already."

The bathroom, at the end of a dark hallway that smelled of mildew, was the coldest room in the house. The tub was half the size of the one at home. The draft coming in through the gap in the north-facing window was intensely cold, making a pleasant contrast with the hot water. I soaked in the bath and scrolled through my phone. I felt uneasy unless I was around my oshi. Over the past few days, the rectangular device had started to feel like my room at home.

There were hardly any pictures of my family and friends in my pictures folder. Organization wasn't my strong suit, and my phone and my laptop were no exceptions, but the photos of my oshi were filed in folders for his child actor, stage, and idol periods so I could pull them up at any time. One of my recent faves was a picture he'd posted to Instagram with the caption < New hair. Decided to go bright. > He'd turned the camera on his reflection in the mirror and thrown up a peace sign, which was cute. He wasn't smiling, but it was a rare pose for him, so he must have been a little excited.

I commented:

< How do you always look so perfect . . . The lighter shade really suits you. Can't wait for the show! >

< Is there some blue in it? Trick of the light? Looks good either way, nice one Masaki. >

< another feast for my eyes thankful for your presence on this earth >

< Sorry to ask but is that shirt from L'Oiseau Bleu?? >

< No way I *just* dyed my hair too? This must be fate lol >

It had been over a year since the incident last July, so the number of positive comments was slowly going up. There were still some die-hard antis, and I was genuinely surprised to see they'd now been following my oshi for longer than his newest fans. It was often fans who turned into antis after some inciting incident, so maybe those were the people responsible for the bashing that was happening now. The anon boards still trailed endless rumors about his relationships with women. Previously, the women being named were models and TV anchors, but recently the victim in that incident when he was supposed to have punched her had been exposed, too. *She wasn't a fan, she was his girlfriend. Management made them keep it under wraps.* When the woman's Instagram was discovered, posters went sleuthing, digging up clues like how there were no selfies from the time of the scandal or that there was a mug in the background that looked like one he had.

I sat on the edge of the tub and put my phone down by the window. There was a soap bottle on the sill, and its spout was crusted over with hair and dust. Diagonal black lines formed diamonds inside the window glass, and beyond it I could see the colors of the fence and the flowers. When you were a celebrity, even a single detail could be identified or turned into a rumor. I climbed out of the tub onto the tile to wash my hair, and as I crouched down, I noticed my body reflected in the tall mirror looking strangely thin. I felt all my strength suddenly drain out through my feet.

✳

When I got back to the living room, the conversation had somehow turned to job searching.

I sank down on the sofa as Mom told me to, and Dad took his place in front of me. Mom cleared the table beside him. Both of them were deliberately creating a heavy atmosphere. I felt bored.

My sister was the only one watching TV, sitting with her legs out to the side and patting her hair dry with a towel. Her ears were red, probably from the warmth of the bath. She was looking the other way, but I sensed she was nervous. My grandmother, who had been a little deaf, had turned on the closed captions on the TV.

"How are you doing these days? Are you looking for a job? How is it going?" Dad asked, hollowly. He put his elbows on the table and crossed his arms. I didn't like him trying to take up space for no reason.

"She isn't. Nothing. I keep telling her. And every time, she lies to me. Lashes out at me, saying 'I did, I did.' It turns out, she called a couple of companies, and that's it. She's not taking it seriously at all."

Mom's eyes widened as she told him. She was more animated than I'd ever seen her. Perhaps it was Dad being here that made her more excited, or maybe it was that my grandmother was gone now. Dad didn't seem to hear her and said, "So how is it?" to me.

"I looked."

"Did you send out any resumes?"

"No, I called them."

"She's not getting anywhere," Mom said again. "Same old story. She always does this. She thinks she can just put it all off."

"You've had six months. Why haven't you done anything?"

"I couldn't," I said.

Mom said, "Liar. You had the time to go to all those concerts."

Yellow foam stuffing was protruding from the black fake leather covering of the couch.

"I know it sounds harsh, but you know we can't keep supporting you forever, either."

I picked at the ruined stuffing with my fingers, and we talked about the future. I turned defiant and demanded the impossible, then suddenly felt a wave of indignance at Dad's patronizing attitude, which came out as a half-laugh by the time it showed on my face. I'd remembered some tweets of his I'd found once, whose comment style had revealed him as a typical boomer. I'd recognized the green sofa in a photo reply to a popular post by a female voice actor and clicked on it assuming it was a coincidence, but the picture was clearly of Dad's apartment.

< Kanamin, I saw your couch and bought the same one
(^_^) Working late and drinking alone before bed
(;^_^)c[_] But I'm back at the grind tomorrow!
Onwards and upwards! >

The last letter was a red exclamation mark image. There were several more posts with similar kaomoji. Dad lived abroad for work, dressed in fancy colored suits and came home from time to time to say cheerful, insensitive things. I'd felt bad for snooping and didn't check the rest of the account. I didn't remember the username anymore, but it made me laugh to think of him directing replies to that voice actor this whole time.

"You still think this is a joke?"

Mom yelled at my smirk, and she got up and started shaking

my arm. My sister's shoulders shot up toward her ears. Pieces of the stuffing I'd been picking at scattered onto the floor.

"Stop, stop," Dad said, and Mom went quiet. Then, muttering some kind of complaint, she went noisily up the stairs. My sister got Mom's phone and followed her.

Something seemed to have changed. Dad seemed to be unbothered.

"If you're not getting a job or going to college, I can't pay your way. Let's decide on a deadline."

Dad spoke logically, in a solution-oriented way. He went on clearly, calmly, and with a smile on his face that belonged to people who found things easy. Everything Dad and other adults said was obvious, and it was nothing I hadn't told myself many times before.

"You've got to work to survive. Just like in the wild—if you can't hunt, you die."

"Then I'll die."

"No, no, that's not what I'm saying."

He tried to placate me while cutting me off, and it got on my nerves. He didn't understand anything. This had to be how Masaki felt. No one understood.

"Then what is it?" I sounded teary. "You keep telling me to work, work. I can't. Don't you know what they told me at the hospital? I'm not normal."

"So you're going to blame it on that again."

"Blame? It's not like, blame, I mean—" I missed a breath, and my throat made a compressed kind of sound. I could see out of the corner of my eye that my sister had come down the stairs, silently, and was standing there. The green color of her T-shirt blurred, and the tears I'd been holding back spilled down my face. I hated that I was crying. I was resentful at my body for dragging me down, for making me cry.

My sobbing sounded louder than I thought it should be.

"Maybe it's fine," my sister said, suddenly. She was looking out the window.

Dad started to say something, but he stopped himself.

"I mean. Isn't it like, enough? Why don't you live by yourself for a while and see how it goes? It's too much, like this."

The sound of water leaking through the roof fell like gentle slaps into the room where we were. The autumn rain was white and cold, slowly destroying our empty home.

In the end, we decided I would move into this house, where my grandmother used to live. I was given money for immediate living expenses, and quit the restaurant. I told my family it was so I could look for a real job, but actually I'd totally forgotten to tell anyone I was out of town, and had gotten a call from Miss Sachiyo.

"I know you've been doing your best, but you know, we're a business, too. I'm sorry, Akari."

A few days ago at the kiosk at the train station, I read an article titled "Masayuki Ueno of Maza Maza Shacked Up with Mysterious Young Beauty? Fan Drift Accelerates." Relationships weren't off limits in his group, and he'd said in an interview that he wanted to get married eventually. The article said, "Fans Furious at Fallen Idol," but I wasn't angry at all. His big sunglasses seemed mismatched with the bags of groceries he was carrying.

I heard a sound like a child screaming in the distance. It seemed to simmer over from deep inside my ears. Noises sounded strangely amplified at dusk. It was almost time for my oshi to go live on Instagram.

I tore open one of the packets of chicken noodles I'd bought in bulk and put the contents in a bowl. Fragments of broken noodle went scattering. Most livestreams, my oshi would be eating, and when he was there, I could at least feel some kind of appetite, so I got everything ready and waited. I rented movies that my oshi recommended, and watched comedians he said were funny on YouTube. When he said goodnight on a late-night broadcast, I went to bed.

I realized that I needed to boil some water. I put the kettle on the stove and put my feet under the musty kotatsu, just as the start of the livestream lit up my phone screen.

My oshi's eyes filled the screen. "Can you see me?" he said. When he pulled back, he was wearing sweats, and he touched his hair, which was a little shorter, with a serious expression that nevertheless had a hint of awkwardness.

Comments started rolling in.

< I can see you! >
< perfect* >
< I'm here >
< hi ev1 >
< We're connected! >

My oshi was moving. Somewhere, right now, he was looking into his phone screen.

< Did you cut your hair? > I entered.

< It's my birthday > someone commented, and after a second my oshi, whose eyes had been swimming, reacted and said, "Today? Happy birthday." The comments kept rolling.

< study break~ it's exam season orz >
< Masaki I found a job!!!! >
< You can call me Yuka* >

My oshi wrinkled his nose, smiling without moving his eyes, but that disappeared instantly into the grainy video, and he quickly raised up a plastic bottle.

"I have Coke. And some delivery on the way. Sushi and salad, plus gyoza."

< Getting fat lol >
< Isn't that service expensive? >
< I use it too, soo handy >

My oshi looked this way with his face propped up on one arm. I could tell from his wavering eyes he was just wondering which comments to react to, but his distracted face was so cute I got a screenshot. I caught him with his eyes closed, so I tried another couple of times, trying to time it right. I noticed the cushion and a stuffed bear on the couch in the background. Unexpected.

He'd mentioned a phobia of fur suits, possibly originating from when he was on a children's educational program when he was young: "I don't know for sure that's where it comes from, but I still can't be around those big animal costumes. I'm not great with stuffed animals, either."

The words were clearly recorded on the sheet of paper filed under "Vulnerabilities" in the binder I'd pulled off the shelf. The doorbell rang, and my oshi said, "Food's here, sit tight," and started to get up. There was a *klunk*, and my vision whirled. His phone must have fallen from wherever it was propped up. I saw an image of a wall and the view through a window.

"Oops," he said, putting it back. "Sorry about that."

It felt like he'd suddenly spoken directly to me, and I felt a little flustered. As the other end of the screen went silent, I heard something through my earbuds. I took them out of my ears. The sizzling sound got louder, and I went to the kitchen and saw the water was boiling over. I shut off the gas and poured the water into a bowl with my left hand, nearly dropping my phone from my other hand. My oshi was back, and he laughed out loud, which was rare. *Crap.* I'd missed whatever it was that had made him laugh. I wanted to skip back, but I wanted to witness the cast in real time, so I'd have to rewatch it later. Technically, maybe there was a lag, but I felt that unlike a CD or a DVD that had been edited, a screen showing a feed that was only a few seconds behind retained some of my oshi's body heat. Outside the window, which I'd closed when I turned the heat on, the stone wall turned dark from the top down in a sudden evening shower.

The box of sushi my oshi showed off when he came back contained nothing but seared salmon, and plenty of people roasted him in the comments. He had a habit of eating only his favorite foods.

< don't u get bored ? >

"I just want to eat food I like," he said, resolutely. "Seared salmon, mmm." He put another piece in his mouth, as though trying to prevent it from breaking into a smile. He insisted on stopping to pick up every last stray grain of rice, falling silent each time. I was in the living room in semidarkness, chewing on a chunk of undercooked noodle. A comment scrolled up the screen.

< Sucking up to fans now that ticket sales are down the drain? >
< Stay in the dumpster where you belong, you flaming piece of trash. >
< Who would even pay to see this loser? Dumb sheeple! >

The same account triple commented, so my oshi couldn't have missed it. He usually let words like these roll off him without batting an eyelid, but this time, in a voice in which the irritation was a few shades darker than on TV or radio, he said, "I don't need any of you to come see the show. We aren't short on fans." He laid down his chopsticks. The comments slowed.

My oshi adjusted the cushions behind him on the couch several times, as if it was his mind he was settling.

"On the other hand," he said, and took a breath, "it is the last one."

The words sounded like they'd been pushed out of his chest. I couldn't fully take them in. Other fans in the comments were also struggling to understand. Maybe it was the lag, but some people were still replying to the anti.

"This probably isn't the right place to tell you, but the announcement's going up on the site soon. So I wanted you to hear it from me first."

My oshi twisted the cap off the Coke with a snapping sound. He tilted it once and drained it to just below the label.

"Leaving? No, it's not just me. We're breaking up."

< Huh? >

< ? ? ? >

< wait wait wait >

< um , >

< NOOOOO! >

A swell of confused comments flowed past in the span of a split second. Among them, some said,

> < And as usual, the world revolves around Little Lord Masaki . . . >
> < Masaki, you're my fave but aren't you being a little selfish? What about your group members?? >
> < Jeez, not before the official account . . . >
> < You should have split up already instead of dragging it out making excuses >

My oshi checked the time and said, "I should save the rest for the presser." He went silent, following the comments, which were scrolling past at incredible speed, and nodding. The nodding didn't seem to be in response to any specific comment.

"No, I'm sorry. But I wanted everyone here to know first. It just never feels like I'm talking to anyone at a press conference. I don't like when things are so one-sided."

> < sry whos bein 1 sided?? >
> < Please can this be fake >
> < Wow feeling kinda abandoned over here haha >
> < So like, announcement tomorrow? >

< i ' m s o b b i n g >

< Did that come out of nowhere or what? I was not. ready. >

"Sorry. I know I'm being self-centered again. I know."

He smiled wryly.

"Thanks for everything—for sticking with a guy like me."

In the midst of the torrent of aggrieved comments, I noticed something different about the way he was talking about himself: *a guy like me.*

He waved and said bye but didn't end the live immediately, reading through the comments instead. He was waiting for something. I wanted to say something, too, but I couldn't find the words. After a while my oshi took a breath, as though to acknowledge there was no good place to stop, and cut the stream.

When it was over, I noticed the rain had stopped. Birds were flying across the sky, away through the sunset. I watched them disappear into the distance over the stone wall and noticed my body had come to a standstill.

The fluorescent lights reflected in each drop of oil floating in the chicken-scented liquid. Bleached scraps of noodles clung to the sides of the bowl. In three days, the liquid would dry and stick to the bottom. In a week's time, it would start to give off a bad smell, which would take a month to fade into the background. Sometimes Mom came and checked on me and made me clean the living room and the kitchen, but the space got dirty again immediately. The floor was littered with objects, and as I made my way across it, a black plastic bag wet with pineapple juice from who knows when stuck to the bottom of my foot. I felt like my back itched, and decided to take a shower. I went out to the garden to get my underwear and pajamas straight from the pole where they were drying, and stopped.

I'd noticed the rain and the laundry, separately, but I hadn't connected them. I didn't know how many times I'd done this since moving here. Pieces of laundry dyed dark by rain jostled on the bowed drying pole, and as I wrung out a bath towel wondering whether I needed to rewash it, the blunt sound of the water hitting the ground echoed through the void inside me. The weight of the water falling on the grass seemed like everything that was pressing on me, and I wrung the whole load out by hand and then left it there. I thought it would probably dry again.

The heaviness still had me in its clutches. I'd been at my grandmother's house for four months. I didn't know where to start looking for a job, and at an interview with a local company I'd randomly found online, I didn't have an answer for why I'd dropped out of high school. I interviewed for part-time jobs as well. They asked me similar questions, and I failed, and I hadn't looked since.

I had the idea to get some Coke and gulp it down to below the label like my oshi, so I put my phone and wallet in my back pocket, grabbed a light down coat, and went out the door. Everyone was walking. Children walked along like they were spraying something from the palms of their mittened hands and played leapfrog with babies in strollers; the older people got, the more they moved parallel to the ground, as if they were carrying something they didn't want to spill. I went down the hill, and the café on the right-hand side was just switching on its "COFFEE" sign. The dark started to set in.

I didn't even have enough coins in my wallet to buy a Coke. Somewhere in the convenience store's big parking lot, by the main road, I could hear a cat mewling. I walked to the ATM and let it swallow my card. It looked like I'd be able to withdraw three thousand yen, but then I must have entered the number wrong because I heard it say, "You have entered an incorrect PIN. Please start again," and this time I typed in my oshi's birth year, carefully. Mom had transferred money into the bank account she had made for me three times before she reached the end of her rope and told me to support myself.

"I'll come over soon." "When are you going to find a job?" "I can't keep doing this."

There was less money this month. But there was still some left. I bought a Coke in the convenience store and gulped it down next to a man who was smoking a cigarette, his shoulders hunched against the cold. The harsh fizz of the carbonation came back up my throat when it should have gone down. I felt my chest bubble and knew winter was no time to be drinking soda. Cigarette smoke seeped into the membrane at the corner of my eye, and my lips let go of the bottle. I looked and saw the liquid was still above the top of the label.

An idol becomes human. I imagined my oshi would say something like, *If you see me in the street, please don't say anything. I'm a normal person now.* He said those words almost verbatim on the news the following afternoon.

The presser looked and felt like a public apology. The whole group was in dark suits, and only their collared shirts, in muted versions of their individual member colors, indicated otherwise. Each camera flash sent my oshi's eyes hazel. There were dark shadows under his eyes. The group bowed, but the angles were all different. Akihito bowed the deepest, while the shallowest bow was from my oshi. Aside from him and Mifuyu, who was already red-faced, the other two kept the corners of their mouths turned up like they were suspended by thread.

Akihito took the mic and said, "Thank you all for being here today."

The questions started. I opened up my notepad and made bullet points down the side: "Moving forward to the next stage." "Positive step for each of us." "Mutual decision." I wrote and wrote, but I couldn't see inside what they were saying. Each group member, separated along a long, white table, would say a few words. It was my oshi's turn.

"...Following this breakup, I, Masaki Ueno, will also be retiring from the entertainment industry. If you see me somewhere in the future, I'd be glad if you could watch over me from a distance, not as an idol, or a performer, but as a private citizen . . ."

His words were so close to what I'd predicted that it wasn't even funny, but what shook me more was the silver ring on the third finger of his left hand. The way he folded his left hand over his right, he clearly had no intention of hiding it, in fact maybe intended it as a kind of silent announcement. The presser wrapped up, leaving behind something about the way he'd said, "I, Masaki Ueno . . ." lodged in my ear like a foreign object.

The breakup, the final concert, and his rumored engagement set the internet ablaze, even more than when he'd gone up in flames. At one point, "My idol's wedding" was even trending.

< Wait wait wait how did this all just happen >

< Mifuyu doesn't look happy about any of this . . . poor girl >

< I always wanted to send my oshi off with a smile but god I just can't stop crying >

< Hold up, that ring? definitely NOT fashion jewelry >

< crashing my oshi's wedding and leaving a cool million in cash as a parting gift >

< Is this guy the reason they're splitting up? >

< Kick him out, problem solved, right? >

< What do you take us fans for?!?!?! After all the ¥¥¥ we
    spent on you?!?! Huh?!? At least have the decency to
    hide it?!?!?!?!? >

< Rap sheet for this flaming piece of trash →→→ Set
    himself on fire assaulting a fan →→→ Leaked group
    retirement ahead of official announcement →→→
    Flaunted suspected engagement at group presser
    →→→ Rumors that fiancée is the assault victim →→→
    Tough time to be a Masaki fan >

< I haven't eaten since I heard been spiraling round and
    round and round and don't understand why he had to do
    this to Akihito when he could have just gotten hitched
    and fucked off? >

< Hey, this just sounds like good news to me. Congrats! >

< Just got told by a former otaku friend at least Sena will
    still be a celeb after the breakup~ :-) um hello your oshi
    is the reason I'll never be able to witness my oshi as an
    idol ever again? :-)) >

< My fellow wotas, you know what this means . . . If we die
    now we could come back as Masaki's kid !!! I shall see
    you all in the next life >

< So he's engaged to that chick he assaulted? For real? >

I felt myself getting drawn into the screen from the tips of my busy thumbs, drowning in the waves of voices. I recalled the time I got lost after school and ended up wandering around Shibuya trying to get to an advance screening of a film starring my oshi. Sneakers, leather shoes, stilettos, and shoes of all shapes and sizes beat down over the blister paving and dirty tiles repeating a mechanical pattern endlessly into the distance. People's sweat and grime encrusted the edges of stairs and pillars piercing vertically through ceilings, and their breath overflowed from the linked boxes of the train cars. People rushed toward escalators that sucked them into buildings with floors stacked on top of one another as if they'd been copied and pasted. People moved inside walls of unthinking repetition. Each post was contained by a rectangular border, with an identical circular profile picture cutout, raging or relishing in the exact same font. My post was one of them, and so was I.

I thought I'd stopped moving, but then suddenly, as if somebody had shoved my shoulder from behind, my eyes stopped on a post. It stood out like the receding back of the person who'd barged into me in the crowd.

< Yikes, he's been doxxed >

I followed the link to the BBS as though I was being sucked in. The origin was a story from a few months ago.

< Just made a delivery to none other than Masaki Ueno >

The post was quickly deleted, but a screenshot made the rounds, and from the poster's comment history, people narrowed down the area where he lived. Then, a cross-reference with the flash of the view outside the window in yesterday's InstaLive identified my oshi's apartment building. It was pretty bad luck that he'd been doxxed right after he'd asked fans to treat him as a private citizen. There were bound to be a few fans who wouldn't be able to resist turning up to try to catch a glimpse of him. If his fiancée was living there, too, there was the possibility of her being harmed in some way, too.

None of the information we'd been given since last night felt real. I could still only feel it on the outside of myself. I was failing to take in the impact of losing my oshi.

I need to give him everything, I thought. *It's all I have.* It was my cross to bear. Believing in him was how I lived. I vowed to put it all on the line for Maza Maza's final concert.

The wind was blowing wildly. The weather had gone quickly downhill as soon as the day had started, and made it dark and damp even inside the concrete walls that enclosed the building. The thunder let out a sound as if it was crashing through the sky, and white flashes exposed the cracks in the walls and the remains of air bubbles in the cement. The head of the snaking line led into the powder room. Inside, colors jostled against white and mirrored walls. Green ribbons, yellow dress, red miniskirt. I thought I made eye contact in the mirror with a woman in blue eyeshadow who was patting foundation under her red-rimmed eyes. Still trailing the thread of her gaze, I went into a stall following the attendant's "Next person, please." My excitement lingered in the tips of my hair where it fell around my shoulders. It flowed swift and smooth and warm behind my ears and made my heart beat restlessly.

From the moment the show started and I heard people start chanting for my oshi, I existed purely to scream his name, to worship him. Second by second, as I followed him and threw up my fists, shouting out the calls and mixes, jumping up and down, the sounds of my oshi's straining breaths rang in my throat, and I felt like I was drowning. I saw him on the jumbo screens, the sweat pouring out of him, and my sides gushed in response. Taking him in awakened my true self. My oshi dragged out of me something I'd given up on—something I normally pushed down and turned a blind eye to for the sake of survival. That was why I had to try to interpret him, to understand. Through getting to know his existence, I tried to sense my own. I cherished the movements of his soul. And when I danced, trying with all my might to catch up with him, I cherished my soul, too. *Shout it out*, my oshi said, with his body, *Shout it loud*. So I did. Like something that was tightly coiled had suddenly been freed and knocked down everything around it, like I was throwing the entire weight of my burdensome life into it, I screamed.

The closer of the first half of the show was a solo number by my oshi. He floated inside the wavering blue light as if he was at the bottom of the ocean, and when he pressed the strings of his guitar with the fingertips of his left hand, the silver glint of his ring looked like something pure and holy. It was just like him not to take it off for the show. He started to sing, almost like he was speaking, and I saw how that boy had grown up into this man. He'd been an adult for a long time now, but I'd only just seen it. Where once he had wailed, "I don't wanna grow up!" he now used his fingers tenderly, as if to caress something. Gradually, the music gained intensity. The bass and the drums joined around him, and he gathered them up with his voice. It was a totally different performance from the one on the album, when he'd seemed to be holding something back throughout. My oshi had taken the heat of the venue, the blue lights, and all our breath into himself and created the song he was singing now from his carmine lips. I felt like I was hearing the song for the first time. Awash in blue light sticks, the Dome containing thousands of people felt tiny. My oshi surrounded us in his warm light.

*

I sat down on the toilet seat. A shiver crawled up my spine. It was like when my body cooled faster after working up a sweat or getting out of a hot bath; after a high, the cold reasserted itself with a vengeance. In the narrow bathroom stall, a pitch-black chill I'd never experienced before rang through my body from deep inside me each time I cast my mind back to just five minutes ago.

It's ending. I adore and cherish and respect him so much, and it's still ending. The four walls of the bathroom stall had cut me off from the world rushing outside. My organs, which I'd felt spasming in the residual excitement, froze over one by one. As the cold slowly spread to my spine, I thought, *No. Please, no.* I pleaded over and over—I wasn't sure to what. *Don't take my backbone from me.* Without my oshi, I really wouldn't make it. Wouldn't know that I was me. My tears felt cold and oily, and my urine spilled out of me and made a vapid sound. I felt alone. The unbearable loneliness made my knees shake.

The woman with the blue eyeshadow was standing near the door out of the bathroom, doing something on her phone. Conscious of her gaze skating over the screen, I tucked my bag under my arm and left, and headed back to my seat. My phone was in the bottom of my bag, still running a voice recording app. I wanted to be back in the heat-filled hall as soon as possible. I wanted my oshi's song to pulse through me forever. I didn't know what I'd do after I'd witnessed his final moments and was left with nothing to hold. Without my oshi, I couldn't be me. My life without him was only an afterlife.

Dear friends,

As I'm sure you all know, the tour finale in Tokyo marked the retirement of my oshi, Masaki Ueno. To be honest, I still haven't come to terms with it yet, since the announcement was so sudden, but I know in the past I've been able to process things through writing here, and more importantly, I'd like to get this down while his image is still fresh in my mind's eye.

For the big day, I went with a total Team Masaki look, with a blue ribbon matched with my favorite blue floral print dress. It's a shame when your oshi's color is blue—even a bright blue only makes you feel colder when it's still coat season. As commonly happens around otaku events, I spotted many girls in coordinated outfits who were clearly of the same persuasion on the train on the way to the Dome, which made me smile. Even though I'd caught the first train of the morning, I found the merch line already waiting for me when I arrived. I got the limited edition light stick, the tour towel, the complete set of photos from the Osaka show, and, for the first time, also the hoodie, T-shirt, wristband (in blue), and hat. I already had the "Best Of" album that was released for the breakup, but the staffer mentioned the version they were selling included a venue-exclusive extra, so I didn't hesitate. Then, several hours later, doors opened, and we went inside. I visited the washroom several times to make sure my makeup was still good (not that anyone was looking). There were five banners in the foyer—red for Akihito, blue for Masaki, yellow for Mifuyu, green for Sena, and purple for Mina—and photos were allowed, so here's mine. Can you see their autographs at the bottom?

Anyway, to get back on topic—I don't need to tell you that my oshi was perfect. There he was, living, breathing, alighting on stage second from left in a sparkly blue sequined costume. He looked like an angel. I was following him through opera glasses, so he was all I could see—he was my world. His cheeks were damp with sweat, and he held them firm and looked ahead with his sharp gaze, and his hair moved, revealing his temples, and I knew he was alive. My oshi was there in front of me. I saw his smile, which can look a little mean because of the way the right side of his mouth lifts higher than the left, and his blinking, which slows tremendously whenever he's onstage, and his fleet footwork that seems to defy gravity completely, and I felt a fever in the marrow of my bones. I knew it was the end.

It was 3:17 a.m. A creeping feeling drifted through my body like the low ringing of a sea cave, and it poked at my stomach, becoming a pain similar to the spasm that came after hunger. The headshot of my oshi I'd brought with me from home loomed pale in the dark, and, strangely, its contours seemed unfamiliar. For the first time, I had the sensation that my oshi, as he currently was, was no longer there. It seemed to me that all photos were in some sense portraits of the dead. Once, years ago, when we went to visit relatives in Kyushu, I got diarrhea from a tangerine I ate from the family altar. The room was laid in new, raw-smelling tatami mats, and when I bit into the tangerine segment my aunt had peeled for me the white sack resisted while the juice inside trickled down my throat, making me feel sick. Perhaps from sitting out as an offering on the altar for so long, it had lost all its sourness; with only sweetness remaining it seemed flat and dull, and I wondered why they bothered putting it on the altar only to eat it later. "What's the point of offerings, anyway?" I said. I don't recall what my aunt said, and I think it was only after I started buying a cake for my oshi's birthday that it made sense to me. I nibbled at my oshi's face on the chocolate plaque nestled in the center of the whipped cream just like I was eating something that had already been placed on an altar. The meaning was in the buying and the sacrifice, and by the time I came to eat it, it was like a gift.

It turned out my secret recording had captured nothing but crowd noise. Thumping footsteps and crying voices obscured everything aside from fragments of singing and faint music. I almost wished I had gotten caught. Nothing felt final. Ever since that day, I'd been hanging around unsteadily, like a ghost that couldn't move on.

The darkness was lukewarm and smelled of decay. I got up to get some water. The constant metallic ring of the refrigerator sounded much louder than usual, intensifying the quietness. I unlocked my phone. The white light of the screen illuminating my face from below was intense, but the night encroaching into the hallway through the garden was stronger. Wanting to push back the border between the light and the dark, I switched on the TV. I started the DVD, which I'd left in the machine. I skipped ahead to 0:52:27, where my oshi had a solo. The image stopped on my oshi looking down, mic in one hand and holding his other arm outstretched. The muscles of his legs, standing solidly on the stage through the white mist, strained toward his center. *He never shrinks*, I thought, and noted this down for the blog. Even through his flowing movements, he held a tension within himself. The feather embellishment by his neckline flipped up, and I could tell by the shifting reflection of its powdery silver edging that his chest was moving up and down minutely. True stillness required a continuous flow of breath and attention directed inward to the center.

It was morning by the time I finished watching. I recognized dawn not by the light, but by a strange floating sensation in my body, which I thought I'd left immersed in darkness. I thought about how the body of a person who drowned eventually floated back up again. I woke up my laptop, which I'd left open, and deleted the line "I knew it was the end."

I typed out "I couldn't believe it was the end," and then, letter by letter, deleted that, too.

When I was stuck for words, I'd take a walk. I went outside carrying only a small bag, and the blue of the clear sky made the backs of my eyelids flicker. With a ballad by my oshi in my earbuds, I found myself at the station. I felt like his music would take me anywhere. A passing train blanketed everything over at an overwhelming volume, and the toes of my blue sneakers caught on the tactile paving and made me stumble. Rocked by the nearly empty train, I looked at my oshi's photos, listened to his songs, and watched clips of his interviews. The oshi who was there belonged to the past.

I changed trains several times and reached his station. There was a bus going in the right direction. Perhaps it was the rough driving, or just my physical state, but the vibrations of the bus jolted my empty stomach and made me feel sick just looking at the blue upholstered seats, so I leaned my body against a window. The bus weaved through the shopping district and between business hotels. My eyes looked out of the window and trailed after red mailboxes, bicycles parked in tangled clusters, and trees along the road that looked dark green and tired from being exposed to the sun. My eyeballs felt restless and I closed my eyelids over them. I felt several impacts as though my cheeks were being punched by the rattling glass, and on one of them, my eyelids parted and I saw the sky, which was now a brighter blue. It seemed to be landing in the backs of my eyes.

"Last stop, please. Time to get off the bus." I heard the driver's monotone call and looked in my belt bag for my pass. As I pulled out my wallet, the pin of a badge that was coming unhooked grazed the back of my hand. The driver said, "Hurry along, please," as though he was addressing the length of the empty bus, and not me. Ejected from the bus, I pressed hard into my trembling legs to keep from collapsing. I was put in mind of the toothpick legs of the cucumber and eggplant animals that were offered up to the ancestors during the August festival.

Once the bus went, I suddenly felt stranded in the residential neighborhood. I sat down on a faded bench that must have once been blue, and holding up my left hand to block the glare, I zoomed in on the app and checked the location. I stood up. I moved toward a sewer hole and heard the sound of running water. I passed another one and heard more flowing. Water was running under the town. I heard the crunch of storm shutters opening and saw dead houseplants in the window of a house. A cat looked in my direction from under a white car, its head lowered. I kept walking, and the streets got narrower. There were side streets and dead ends I hadn't noticed when I checked my phone. I thought there might be a way through that wasn't on the map, so I shoved past cars pushing out from garages, trampled over weeds in vacant lots, and broke through an apartment block's bicycle parking area, and then I reached an open space.

I was at a river. A rusty guardrail stretched along it into the distance. I walked for a while until I felt my phone vibrate to tell me I had reached my destination. The guardrail ended, and an apartment building stood on the other side of the river.

It was a normal apartment building. I couldn't see its name, but I was pretty sure it was the same one that had been posted online. Having come here without a plan, I stood and looked at it for a while. It wasn't that I wanted to see him.

Suddenly, someone drew the curtains in the window of the room in the upper right, and the balcony door slid open with a groan. A woman with a bob cut came stumbling out with a load of laundry, leaned it against the handrail, and sighed.

Our eyes nearly met. I looked away. I walked on, acting as though I had just been passing, moving faster and faster until I was running. I didn't know which apartment was his, and I didn't care who the woman was. It didn't matter if he didn't live in that apartment building at all.

What had undeniably hurt was the load of laundry in her arms. One shirt or a pair of socks could speak more about a person's current existence than all the binders, photographs, and CDs in my room I'd worked so hard to amass. I came up against the fact that there was someone there who'd continue to witness my oshi in real time even now that he was gone.

I couldn't keep following after him. Now that he was no longer an idol, I could no longer keep watching him, trying to understand him. My oshi had become a man.

I was still skating around the question of why he'd hit someone. It had been on my mind the whole time, but I knew I wouldn't find the answer to that by peering in from outside that apartment. There was no way for me to know. His sharp glare back when it all started hadn't only been directed at the media. It was a look that said it was the two of them against the rest of the world.

I ran and ran, until I came to a cemetery. The gravestones stood peacefully in the sun. The shed I passed near the entrance had a tap, and brooms and buckets and ladles were propped up beside it. Offertory flowers were scattered around, severed at the stems. The flowers smelled like open wounds. It reminded me of the smell of bedsores I knew from my grandmother's sickbed. Suddenly, I remembered the day she was cremated. A body, on fire. Flesh burned and turned to bone. When my grandmother made Mom stay in Japan, Mom kept telling her that it served her right. Mom had grown up hearing from my grandmother how she was no daughter of hers. Mom had cried and said, "Now you want me to stay and be your daughter." Consequences. Your own actions coming back to you. I'd believed it was my purpose in life to devote myself to my oshi, to give up my flesh for bone. That was how I'd wanted to live. But now, now that I was dead, I had no way of gathering my own bones out of the ashes.

I got lost, repeatedly, got on the wrong bus, and almost dropped my pass. By the time I got to my station it was two o'clock. I got home. All that greeted me there was reality—clothes strewn where I'd thrown them, hair ties, chargers, plastic bags, empty tissue boxes, an upturned bag. Why couldn't I live normally? Manage to do the bare minimum needed to be human? I never meant to break things, make a mess of them. I tried to live, but things just kept piling up like the waste from my own body. I tried to live and my home collapsed around me.

I didn't know the truth of why my oshi hit another person,

why he tried to destroy with his own hands something he valued. Would never know. But somewhere on a deeper level, I felt connected to it. That moment—when he forgot about the public gaze, unleashed the power that he'd been holding back in his eyes, and tried, for the first time, to break something—was coursing through my body. I'd lived with my oshi's shadow on me for so long, always carrying double the breath, double the body heat, double the yearning. I saw the crying twelve-year-old boy with his shadow torn off by a dog. I'd been burdened by the weight of the flesh of my body ever since I'd been born. Now, I wanted to heed its trembling and destroy myself. I wanted to do it myself, instead of letting it happen to me. My gaze ran over the table. It caught on a canister of cotton swabs. I grabbed it, and flung my arm upward. The tension in my abdomen bolted up my spine, and I breathed in. My vision went wide and turned the color of meat. I swung my arm down. I swung down with all my might, like I was slamming down all of the anger and regret I was holding for the person I had been.

The plastic canister made a noise as it rolled away. The cotton swabs scattered.

*

The crows were cawing. I gazed around at the room for some time. Every corner of it was exposed in the light entering from the veranda and through the window. I realized that I'd made it all—not just the center, but the whole. The bones and the meat, it was all me. I thought back to the instant before I'd thrown my fist. The dirty glass, the bowl still full of broth, the remote control. I'd cast my eye over them and chosen the cotton swabs which were the simplest to clean up. Laughter rose in me like a bubble, then burst with a pop.

I started picking up the cotton swabs. On my knees, head down, as carefully as if I were gathering the bones out of somebody's ashes, I picked up the cotton swabs I had cast on the floor. Once I'd retrieved them all, I'd still need to clean up the moldy old rice balls, and the empty bottles of Coke, but now I could see the long, long road ahead.

Crawling on my hands and knees, I knew I'd found a way to keep living.

Trying to stand on my own two feet hadn't worked out, but I could go forward like this for now. My body felt heavy. I picked up a cotton swab.

AFTERWORD

An idol burns. I'm not talking about a celebrity physically going up in flames. It's about someone in the public eye who commits a misdeed or makes an improper remark, and becomes the target of criticism, is scrutinized from every angle, and loses their influence. When did we start using the words "*enjō suru*" and "*moeru*" for this sight? And are there words that correspond to these in other languages? In Japanese, "enjō suru" and "moeru" fundamentally point to similar phenomena, but today they are used in slightly different ways. There's a reason I used the verb "moeru" and not "enjō suru" at the start of this story: "My idol is *on* fire," rather than "my idol is *under* fire." While "enjō suru" is almost only used with regard to celebrity scandals, "moeru" is also routinely used for objects on fire. In the opening line of the novella, I chose to use "moeru" so that in addition to the correct meaning of the oshi being involved in a scandal, there's also an echo of the literal sense of something burning. So that way, the cruelty of the word—deployed to describe the image of an idol's body catching on fire and burning up—is immediate to the reader.

Yes, flaming is cruel. The criticisms can be right or wrong, depending on the case, but a person burning is always cruel. I say that the criticisms can be right or wrong because criticism is sometimes warranted. Politicians who make a discriminatory remark, for example, should be properly criticized. If they were to face no consequences for their actions, there is a chance even more people will get hurt. But, that being said, even those politicians have a private life and a family. For example, the son of a politician who enrolled at my school. As soon as he started, he was teased and bullied for having the same last name as the politician. I heard students in his year talking about this with glee, and it made me feel dizzy. I got angry at them. The boy had done nothing wrong, but at the time, the bashing against the politician became so intense and so personal that it made stupid and ignorant middle schoolers think it was okay to bully him. People online made his dad into a laughingstock, but this was many years ago, so if you were to talk about him on social media now, I don't think there would be much of a reaction. In the case of baseless defamations, of course, but also in cases where the person lost their position because the criticism was justified, the flames consumed both the individual in question and their innocent family members. This is why I believe that all flaming is cruel, whether or not criticism is warranted.

This novella is a story about a girl who supports an idol who goes up in flames after he hits one of his fans. It's not clear why he did it, nor whether he's a good person or not. It's also unclear whether the criticism directed at him is accurate or not. She never finds out. Of course, a fan isn't in a position to know these things, but Akari continues to be hurt by her idol's scandal, which she doesn't fully understand. Having made her idol her purpose in life, and having relied on him for emotional support, she, too, is consumed by the cruelty of the flaming.

Sometimes the thing in life you depend on is suddenly subjected to some kind of baffling, cruel calamity. What can you do when that happens? When the only thing you believe in, the one thing that helps you survive, is lost, how do you think about it, and what do you do? I'm thankful that this book being translated into English allows people to read it whom I wouldn't otherwise be able to talk to. I hope there's something in it that speaks to you.

ACKNOWLEDGMENTS

For my brother . . .

I borrowed my experience of helping you study English for the scene in this story featuring the "third person -*s*." You'd recognize it, of course, without me needing to say so. (Although our family was nothing like the family of this novella, and I was a far more sanctimonious sister than tenderhearted Hikari.) You seemed to have been born with a runny nose, and never seemed to find the motivation to study. You struggled with kanji, and I remember you sitting in front of worksheets, wiping your nose with the palm of your hand, claiming it was stopping you from being able to do your homework, and getting scolded. I always wondered why you didn't just do it. Back then, no one—not even you yourself—understood about people who have trouble learning kanji or doing things the way most people do them. In elementary school I worried, and would often try to check on you from the hallway. One of these times, I saw pictures posted on the wall opposite your class-room, of different imaginary trees. Your classmates had drawn fancy trees with ribbons, trees with rainbow apples, trees laden with red apples. Among these, there was one picture that was unlike the others, with your name on it. Entitled "RINNE" (as in reincarnation), your drawing must have been influenced by Osamu Tezuka's *Buddha*, but also looked like van Gogh's *Starry Night*, though of course through child's eyes: dark, gnarled trees stood within a muddy ochre atmosphere that seemed to portend a storm, surrounded by swirls of green, brown, and dark red. Having only ever thought of you as an easygoing child, I had the sense then of having come into contact with something unfathomable within you.

But even after that, I didn't try to appreciate you. I didn't make a habit of criticizing you, at least, but there was one day that, just like the older sister in this story, I told you, "You don't need to try. Just stop *pretending* you're trying." Time passed, and I forgot I'd ever said such a thing. As I came up against my own troubles, and you came up against yours, perhaps it became the least of our problems. In time, I finally gained a little perspective and started sticking up for you, as though to make up for my past actions.

Much later, I took a college psychology class in which we were instructed to write おはようございます in mirror writing. Writing backwards takes longer than writing the normal way.

Acknowledgments

The letters don't come out as neatly, and mainly it takes a lot of effort. I imagined needing to put in extra work all the time, as though you were writing backwards when everyone around you was writing normally. Then showing someone what you'd worked so hard to achieve with your unsteady hand, only for it to be taken for granted and them to say, "I knew you could do it if you tried." Having to write backwards your whole life, with no one even noticing—maybe this was your experience of the world. I know I owe you an apology. On behalf of the characters who stood in Akari's way, to make up for having caused hurt that can't be taken back.

Not being a reader of novels, you'll probably never read this book, or this note for the English translation. But when you found out I wanted to be a writer, you dropped by the bookstore and chose a story that was then up for the Akutagawa Prize to give to me as a present. I carefully read each line, and cried. That piece didn't end up winning, but a few years later, I became a published author, and won the Akutagawa with this novella. Becoming a writer gave me a way to live. You transferred to a different school and developed your own way of learning, different from the conventional Japanese system, and now you're top of your class, getting perfect scores on tests. From crawling on the floor, you clawed your way to a new life. You don't need to make yourself do what you can't do. There's nothing wrong with you, or Akari. It was the things that invalidated you—society, institutions, me that day—that were in the wrong. Your world, which was stifled by our education system, is still, in spite of it, as vibrant as those trees I saw in the hallway of our elementary school. May happiness be yours, brother. And may the light shine, both for you back then, and for you in the future.

A NOTE FROM THE TRANSLATOR

Sometimes I think about translating as the act of making something in one language accessible to people using another. Lately, though, I've been pondering the idea of translating for readers who can also read the original. Granted, that limits my imagined audience quite a bit. But in some ways, this doesn't seem as strange an idea as it sounds.

For instance: you might not speak Japanese, but maybe you're interested in the idol scene, or in anime. Maybe you have another fandom, or something else you invest with the most hopeful parts of yourself. Maybe you just enjoy saying things on the internet.

I was surprised by how easily I seemed to be able to imagine how the social media comments in this book would sound in English. Each corner of the internet has a different culture and set of conventions, but the gestures, dynamics, and narratives that arise out of the collective are only too familiar. Little wonder, perhaps, because these are many of the same platforms that cultivate this behavior in the Anglophone social media space. Can't you almost hear their voices on the screen?

At the same time, online is a deeply visual language where spelling, punctuation, and non-word elements are all active signifiers. Akari cringes at her father's use of the red exclamation mark emoji. I was concerned that all the commentary perhaps came across a little more pointed in my English than it does in the Japanese: Part of the value of literary fiction is that it doesn't simply reproduce the language we encounter in other parts of life. But if we think of Japanese as the origin of visual elements like emoji and kaomoji, it makes sense that English looks more extreme when it expands into that online space. And, as Akari points out, fandom talk can get a little overheated.

As I translated this book, I thought about why Akari feels so much more at home talking to other fans online than she does trying to express herself to her teachers or her parents. I tried to hear how she speaks to herself, how she writes to followers of her blog, how she comes across to adults. In a way, it's her sensitivity to context that is paralyzing.

Beset by overwhelming sensory information, she entrusts a lot of her physicality to the figure of Masaki: charismatic, complex, larger than life. But it's also this sensitivity that allows her to learn to offer him what she herself needs. She can fly, and eat, and face the reality of her circumstances because she's helped him do the same. Sometimes it's hard to trust that felt experience can be communicated whatever the language used. But I keep translating.

As armed conflict in Ukraine once again invokes the specter of nuclear war, it seems apposite to also acknowledge the ghosts that populate the backdrop of this book. The images of flashes of light and bodies on fire; shadows, sloughing skin, and burned bones. And—above all—a man confronted by a force greater than that which he has wielded, and conceding his own mortality and humanity in the face of it.

Masaki's birthday, August 15, was the date that the Showa Emperor informed the nation in 1945 of the surrender of Japan's armed forces, citing the atomic bombs that were dropped on Hiroshima and Nagasaki. Under the subsequent US occupation, he made a declaration in which—according to some commonly held interpretations, particularly those based on the official English translation—he renounced his divinity. Another interpretation says he never claimed to be a god in the first place.

His son and successor Akihito, the Heisei Emperor, abdicated the throne in 2019, ushering in a new era named Reiwa. This book, Usami's second, came out in 2020, when she was twenty-one, and was the single bestselling novel published in

Japanese that year. A strange and memorable year for many of us.

The image of the dry white pieces of bone that remain after a body is cremated may be unfamiliar to some readers. Did you ever use a handful of cotton buds to craft a skeleton keychain? Me neither, to be honest. But if you ever end up disillusioned or at a dead end and needing to find your way back to yourself, it could be as good a place to start as any.

—*Asa Yoneda*

ABOUT THE AUTHOR

Born in 1999, Rin Usami was raised in Kanagawa Prefecture, just outside of Tokyo, and began writing novels in high school. Her debut novel, *Kaka*, won the 56th Bungei Prize and the 33rd Yukio Mishima Prize. For her second novel, *Idol, Burning*, Usami received the prestigious Akutagawa Prize—making her the third-youngest recipient in the award's history. She is currently an undergraduate student at Waseda University in Tokyo.

ABOUT THE TRANSLATOR

Asa Yoneda is the translator of several books from Japanese, including *Dead-End Memories* by Banana Yoshimoto, and *The Lonesome Bodybuilder* by Yukiko Motoya, which was a finalist for the 2019 Otherwise Award. She grew up in Japan, the UK, and the US, and now lives in Bristol, England. Between translations, she has worked as a maître d', a public library manager, and a spy, among other jobs.

A NOTE ON THE COVER AND INTERIOR ART

A NOTE ON THE COVER

In creating the cover imagery for *Idol, Burning*, the use of color and repetition were implemented to convey an overwhelming sense I envisioned for the story. Utilizing the collected objects in a stacked display style, I focused on allowing the items to balance, teetering on collapse. The frame of the image concedes little breathing room, as obsession with another has become the focus of life. Rin Usami's brilliant sketches of fixation and energy are relayed in the portrayal of an image on the brink of crashing.

—*Delaney Allen*

A NOTE ON THE INTERIOR ART

When creating illustrations for the book, I really wanted to try to capture the quiet moments of loneliness that Akari experiences. Rin Usami was able to write about Akari's feelings of hopelessness in a way that felt tender and real. Her extreme fandom is rather unassuming, and her slow descent into the only thing that brings her comfort is such a stark contrast to other portrayals of idol fans. Although I've never felt the way Akari did about an idol, the vividness of Usami's descriptions of Akari's deterioration left me thinking about the book for days after I read it. I truly appreciated this compassionate and thoughtful view of something that may be completely incomprehensible to those outside of it.

—*Leslie Hung*

Here ends Rin Usami's
Idol, Burning.

The first edition of the book was printed and
bound at LSC Communications
in Harrisonburg, Virginia, October 2022.

A NOTE ON THE TYPE

The text of this novel was set in Freight Text Pro, originally designed in 2005 by Joshua Darden—the first African American type designer, according to *Fonts in Use*. The Freight font superfamily is known for its innovative approach to optical size and stylistic versatility, and Freight Text Pro provides its sturdy center. Aptly named, Freight is a workhorse font that can handle standard text sizes for small and large amounts of copy. Unique but easy on the eyes, Freight is a go-to typeface for everything from magazines to cookbooks to data-driven documents.

HarperVia

An imprint dedicated to publishing international voices,
offering readers a chance to encounter other lives and other
points of view via the language of the imagination.